ONE VERY HOT DAY IN A DIRTY WAR...

"You came to save us, you Americans," Thuong said.

"Not to save, to help," Lieutenant Anderson said.

"No, save, save is the better word, but I am afraid, Lieutenant, that you will find that we are not an easy people to save."

For once Anderson did not protest, and Thuong continued, his voice lower, his eyes almost closed, speaking as though he were talking to himself, "We can not even save ourselves. That is the worst thing. We can not save ourselves. I am sorry."

"Halberstam can now add the successful-novelist cluster to his distinguished war-correspondent medal."
—*Library Journal*

ONE VERY HOT DAY

DAVID HALBERSTAM

WARNER BOOKS

A Warner Communications Company

PS
3558
A34
O53
1984

This Warner Books Edition is published by arrangement with
Houghton Mifflin Co.

Portions of this book have appeared in *The Saturday Evening
Post*.

Warner Books, Inc.
666 Fifth Avenue
New York, N.Y. 10103

 A Warner Communications Company

Printed in the United States of America

First Warner Books Printing: June, 1984

10 9 8 7 6 5 4 3 2 1

FOR ELZBIETA

Chapter One

THE SEMINARY was outside of the little town. But the priests were all gone now, gone back to Europe. The Seminary now had massive fortifications, no enemy would storm it easily, miles and miles of barbed wire, mountains of sandbags, and on top a Vietnamese machine gunner, sometimes awake. By the gate there was a sentry and a huge sign which said: "Welcome. Eighth Infantry Division U.S. Advisory Group. Best There Is." Under that was a caricature of an American officer with a huge grin, and then the initials W E T S U. There was no printed explanation for the initials but translated verbally to those who asked, civilians largely, they meant, We Eat This Shit Up.

Beaupre lay there asleep, a thin uncomfortable sleep, the sweat rolling off him, the giant fan above him no help, serving only to distribute equally the very hot air. He was so uncomfortable that when they sent someone to get him his nerves were already jarred, and he was instantly sure that they wanted him to go to war: that the night had passed, it was time for the operation. Volleyball, he heard dimly. *Volleyball.*

"Hey Captain Beaupre. Volleyball?" They had sent a young Captain for him. Beaupre did not even know his name.

"No," he managed to say. "Jesus no, volleyball."

"They sent me to get you. We need a man. We've got nine. The others say you're supposed to."

"Do I look like I'm supposed to?" It was a good question: he was thirty-eight, looked older, heavy, almost fat; he was sweating without playing; he breathed and he sweated. "The U.S. government spent sixteen hundred dollars to get me out here and it never said anything about volleyball."

"We need a man," the Captain said doggedly; he was young and new at the Seminary and he had been preceded by impressive rumor-mongering. It was said he would make the early list for major.

"You need a boy," Beaupre corrected.

"Colonel says volleyball's the exercise. You need it. We all need it."

"I don't need it," Beaupre said. "I'm lazy. The rest of you get too much exercise."

Jesus, Beaupre thought, volleyball. Five o'clock in the afternoon and they were out there playing goddamn volleyball. They all played volleyball at the Seminary because there was nothing else to do. Grown men. Beaupre could hear them now in the background, shouting and grunting. It was the only thing to do and besides the Colonel liked it, and was good at it, the Colonel, small and wiry, saw himself as a feeder, very fast. The Colonel wasn't there, he was in Saigon, due back that night, the Colonel, lover and founder of the game;

when they lacked a man, the Colonel would come into Beaupre's room and drag Beaupre out, making a small and almost pleasant spectacle of it, boasting, *Look who wants to play,* and Beaupre, dutifully requisitioned, would play, summoned only to even the sides, lunging gracelessly from the start, grunting loudly, in all a small and gentle humiliation.

He had come to hate volleyball and he had gained a kind of private vengeance against them all when they had played the Vietnamese officers. The Vietnamese liked volleyball too, and the Colonel heard of this, and always anxious to improve relations had suggested a game of Us-against-Them. The Vietnamese officers accepted the invitation, perhaps a bit too readily, and the Colonel was very pleased. The Americans, prepared to be good winners, had fixed a giant barbecue for later. The Viets had come and played, thin, often scrawny men, odd in their much too long shorts, ludicrous in their old-fashioned undershirts (they were more modest than the Americans and did not strip to the waist). Seeing the Vietnamese and the tall powerful Americans, Beaupre had felt rare sympathy for the Viets. The game began and the Americans took a quick lead. When the Viets finally made some points the Americans very carefully applauded; this applause stopped when the Viets, old undershirts and all, made a quick work of the Americans. Five games were played and won, ever more handily; by the end there was clapping for American points. It had been an embarrassing day; the Vietnamese behaved well and were careful not to throw the last game; the barbecue had gone reasonably well, but there had never been any suggestion of a rematch. Indeed for a time it dampened volleyball fever, but after a week, the Colonel, resilient as ever, had bounced back and reinstituted the American game.

Beaupre listened to the game now; the briefing would be late that night after the Colonel returned. There would be a movie first. He had five hours before the briefing and yet if he slept, he would only feel worse later on. It was a tribute to how much he had come to dislike volleyball that despite the suffocating boredom of the Seminary he refused to watch them play; he tried to sleep a little more before the movie.

The volleyball game was over and they were still waiting for the Colonel. He was due back a little later, driving back on the country's one highway against the orders of Saigon which disliked and distrusted the highway and thought he should take a helicopter; it would be very embarrassing if a Bird Colonel were ambushed and killed within forty miles of the main city. But the Colonel did not like Saigon, and rarely if he could help it, listened to it; he did like what he called looking at the countryside, and trying to find out who was in the lead. So while they waited for him at the Seminary they decided to show the movie first. Usually the movies were of Elvis Presley in Hawaii, or Doris Day in bed with someone, her pajamas unwrinkled, and her hair all in place, and the main excitement would come with Doris in bed, her teeth already brushed, when a lizard would start crawling across the wall which served as a screen. Someone, usually Raulston, would shout out what the lizard was about to do, and there would be great encouragement for the lizard, *go to it old buddy,* and some disappointment if the lizard backed off, *that lizard can't cut the mustard,* and *tell him where to go Beaupre* (in honor of Beaupre who was acknowledged the resident swordsman). Sometimes there would be another lizard, probably female, and thus in the middle of a cowboy film, or a Doris Day in Bed film, the attention would shift to the two lizards doing their ballet on the screen, with cheers for the male lizard, though Raulston who claimed to have studied biology insisted that they were all wrong, the aggressor lizard was the lady, and they were cheering the wrong lizard. On this night while they waited for the Colonel, they did not have Elvis or Doris, and the lizards were in the off season, but they had *The Guns of Navarone,* which as someone said was still playing in New York, yes said someone else, Watertown, New York. But it was still first run by their standards, their standards being whatever the Army sent down, which was what the Saigon officers did not choose to take. It was a fine movie filled with action and handsome mountains and beautiful color and Gregory Peck and Anthony Quinn on the same side, though not trusting each other. It went very well until someone discovered Peck's defection and shouted: "He's a damn VC."

There was a slow sense of shock when he said it, and then slowly it dawned on everyone that it was true, that Peck was a Cong, and from then on the complexion of the picture changed sharply, and the loyalty to Peck ended abruptly, the hearts did not beat so fast when the Germans came near, and the beautiful girl, seemingly loyal to Peck, then step by step obviously betraying him, in the movie a fink, now a loyal government agent, drew occasional cheers. From then on they shouted encouragement to the German sentries, and when Peck and others repeatedly slipped by the sentries, Raulston ordered one of the sergeants out of the mess hall where the movie was being shown to check the perimeter and make sure that no Vietcong had slipped past the sentries. When the Sergeant came back and said that one of the Vietnamese sentries had been asleep there was more laughter, which like the game they were now playing with the movie, eased the tension. On the screen the Germans, tipped off on the whereabouts of Peck and the others, were arresting them in the market. There was some cheering, but someone, sensing that it was too early in the movie for Peck to die or disappear, shouted: "Don't take any prisoners." Peck did escape and continued bravely on, putting down the revolt among the civil libertarians in his own group. Steadily they passed obstacle after obstacle, finally entering the guerrilla-proof gun batteries and, miracle of miracles, silencing the guns.

"Hell of a good movie," said Lieutenant Anderson, as they walked out.

"Yes," said Captain Beaupre, annoyed to find how little pleasure he had gotten, annoyed to find that Vietnam took the pleasure even out of Gregory Peck killing Germans.

Beaupre checked his watch and saw that they had time for a drink before the briefing. "Buy this old man a drink," he said to Anderson. They went to the bar and ordered one drink; Anderson did not want it very much, particularly he did not want it before the briefing, but in six months he had received few enough invitations to be with

Beaupre to turn any down. While they were drinking, the Chaplain came over and appeared to drink with them (appeared to drink because Beaupre had long suspected that the Chaplain, who drank beer from the can, disliked alcohol and nursed one drink throughout the evening). The Chaplain was always at the bar, though never drunk, always the first to laugh at the dirty jokes, though never telling any himself. Beaupre almost felt sorry for him (which was a lifting of his general ban on chaplains) trying so hard to be one of the boys. It was a difficult war to be a chaplain in: the Americans here were mostly officers and older men, and the war itself was not yet hairy enough to drive them into the arms of a chaplain; the Chaplain spoke somewhat nostalgically about Korea and the type of army they had then. Beaupre told Anderson to buy the Chaplain a drink, saw both of them embarrassed, because Anderson was still young enough and innocent enough to be embarrassed by the Chaplain's presence at the bar. It was a scene which pleased Beaupre, the one golden young officer not wanting to buy a beer for the other who didn't want to drink it. It made the time pass faster for him, and he went out of his way to be polite to the Chaplain for the next half hour. He deliberately talked about Korea and how tough that was, and the Chaplain joined in. He had never been particularly nice to the Chaplain before, and he knew this made the Chaplain a little uneasy. It amused him until they were summoned for the briefing.

The briefing made an odd scene, most of the men now on their way to bed, clad only in towels wrapped around them and Japanese shower shoes. Their physiques alone told much of the story of the changing army: the young ones, lean and hard and anxious to go, the older ones, in two wars already, showing some of the softness of the long years of peace and peacetime army diet, flabby around the middle. Most of them wore their professional tans: very red faces and fore-arms, and pale white elsewhere; only a handful of physical culturists, most of them in noncombat roles, had real tans; those who had to live and work under the Delta sun did not seek it on their days off. The Colonel was singularly white, even his neck was white; Beaupre had sometimes won-dered how, he walked through operations, he had every chance to burn like everyone else, but he remained white. As a group they liked and trusted the Colonel, and he was popular for lying to them as little as possible; he was an easy man to read, direct and quick to anger; he was, Beaupre could tell, not happy about the day in Saigon, and not happy about the operation.

He outlined, with a map and a pointer, the objective: a reported Vietcong rest house on a route traversing the area. "The Ho Chi Minh motel," someone said, a used, but still popular joke.

"How good's the intelligence, sir?" someone asked.

"The Vietnamese," he said, drawing the word out, very slowly for emphasis so that the word wasn't Vietnamese at all, it was *they,* "seem to think it's good enough." Someone laughed. That was why they liked him.

"Did we participate in the planning?" someone asked.

"Did we participate in the planning?" the Colonel repeated, again deliberately. His face screwed up.

"In a way. There were other places our friends wanted to go instead, places where we suspected the enemy did not exist and indeed had never heard of." A pause for their smiles. "We expressed a preference for places where according to our photo reconnaissance the enemy is putting down rather solid defensive structures, and so we compromised on this, although Captain Donovan of our intelligence informs me that he suspects that this was the place where our friends wanted to go in the first place. I suspect that Captain Donovan's suspicions are correct." Laughter. The Colonel, hearing it, smiled a polite little smile of his own pleasure; he was a modest man, more like a schoolteacher than a Colonel, and his manner and his tartness told Beaupre that the Colonel knew finally that he would never be a general, and that his wife would never be a general's wife; the Colonel, Beaupre gathered, had not been considered that much of a wit five years before.

He began slowly to explain the operation. Three prongs. Two walking in. One flying in on helicopters, coming in after the others had moved. The villages they would touch. "Who will fly tomorrow," said the Colonel, "who will be the glory leader and have his photograph taken jumping out of the helicopters?"

Beaupre sat in the briefing and waited, hoping he looked impassive: perhaps, he thought, they will think I want it. He didn't want the helicopters and he didn't want the reserve force, which sat there by the CP and worked only when there was contact, and was dropped in, more often than not into a specially prepared second ambush; he wanted the ground troops. He looked around him and saw the other faces; some of them, the younger ones, eager, some impassive. Perhaps the impassive ones, he thought, want the helicopters too but are too proud to show it. Beaupre was a little older and probably a little more frightened than most. He watched the Lieutenant next to him, *his* lieutenant, the most eager face there. The Lieutenant wanted the helicopters; he liked the assault.

"Let me pick a hero," the Colonel said, his eyes wandering around the room. There was a brief pause. The Colonel enjoyed the drama of this. "Redfern, Captain Redfern," he said. Redfern was Captain William Redfern known to all of them and particularly to himself as Big William. "You ready with those Rangers, Redfern?"

"Big William and his Rangers always ready. Fact is, Colonel sir, they'd have hurt feelings they knew you asked a question like that, and maybe Big William even lose a little face with his Rangers."

"I don't like my men to lose face, Redfern, so you pass on my respects to them."

"Big William glad of that, sir, it hurt them Rangers somethin' awful, their man lose face."

He came from Pickens, Alabama, a huge giant of a Negro, a certified graduate, he said, of Snake Oil Tech—it even said Big William on his certificate, he claimed. He said he was supposed to get a pro football tryout but failed because Uncle Jim didn't want him to play; Uncle Jim who, someone asked him; Uncle Jim Crow, Senior, he said, what other Uncle Jim is there? But Uncle Jim too smart to keep Big William from trying out for the Army, that his way of making it all up to me. Big William was not polite, not cautious, not sensitive whose ears his boasts fell on; he was black as black can be, *they* never integrated with *his* family, he said; he walked with a sort of rolling sexual grace, and he always carried an ivory swagger stick which he used as if both to emphasize his grace and his color; his record player, oblivious to other men, and other tastes, ran constantly, blaring out dark-sounding sensuous music; oh, and he talked endlessly, about his women, boasted constantly about them, made it clear they were not all black as black can be, and proclaiming the "finest piece of equipment south of Sagion, white, black or yellow, excluding the Vietcong because I ain't fraternized with any of their women yet, at least knowingly I ain't." Not all these qualities were endearing, and there were constant arguments at the Seminary on how good Big William really was. Some of the younger officers liked him (and his music), were awed by his size, and accepted Big William's evaluation of himself. He was, the younger ones sometimes said, the best Negro officer they had ever seen; the others, older, particularly Raulston, said he was like all the rest of *them*, a bullshitter, the only difference was that he talked more, longer and louder than the others; you just don't know them, Raulston said, I've seen them all, and he ain't the best, they don't have a best, but maybe he's the worst, they got that. (The Colonel, pressed for an answer to this, for a solution one hot night when a private committee had arrived to complain about Big William's record player, only his record player, had said, "Oh, yes, he's a bullshitter, no doubt of that, never saw an officer boast as much as that one. Boasting isn't good for an officer and I don't want the rest of you trying it. Still he's a hell of a good officer. Funny thing is, he doesn't know it yet himself. He's too busy acting it out. Probably happened to him accidentally. He's not the best officer I have, not by a long shot, but he might be the best adviser. He's number one with the Vietnamese. They eat it up. Even the music.") Which was true: the Vietnamese were in awe of him, his size, his color, his great deep voice, and he seemed to come alive in their presence, they were his very own kingdom. Each morning he would greet them: "Good morning, Vienamese," he would say, and they would answer in a chant he taught them, "Good morning, Big William." "How they hanging, Vienamese?" he would ask and they would answer, their voices thin like school children, "They hanging fine, Big William."

"I keep getting reports that the Rangers are losing their meanness and becoming civilized. Is this true, Big William?" the Colonel was saying.

Big William shook his head like someone who has just been libeled and can't understand why. "Beg your pardon, but that ain't shit, Colonel sir. Big William watches them Rangers close, and he guarantees them nasty as ever. I catch them bein' gentlemen and I kickass special for you. Big William pass on what you said though, sir."

"All right, Captain Redfern, you take the helicopters and the heliborne assault." Anderson's face showed obvious disappointment. Beaupre looked across the room to see if there were any sign on Big William's face, but there was just a small sign that the Rangers and their adviser had received their just due. "And Big William," the Colonel added, "make them go, make them shagass." The Negro nodded, "They goin' to fly tomorrow, Colonel, we won't even need the helichopters, them chopters only slow us down. You want us to shag, we goin' to shag by the numbers for you." Until Big William's arrival the Rangers had always bewildered the Americans. They were supposed to be elite troops like the Marines and the Airborne, but they were not particularly effective and had regularly disappointed the Americans. (Donovan, the intelligence chief, claimed it was because they were elite in a different sense, troops turned over by regular units on the demand of officialdom, but not the best, and not the worst, simply, according to Donovan, the most disorderly and unmanageable.)

"Captain Beaupre," the Colonel said, "suppose you walk in from the east. See if you can't restrain your tiger from joining battle too often with the enemy along the way." The Colonel got more laughter on this because everyone enjoyed the fact that Beaupre who was sour and often bitter had been switched to Dang, who was considered the worst of the Vietnamese officers.

Afterward, after the Colonel had strung out the drama as best he could and done a brief flash of an impersonation of Saigon, enough to amuse them but not quite enough to be improper (How's your war down there in the Delta, Harrison? Just fine sir. That's good Harrison, keep up the good work), they broke up. Anderson had lingered for a moment and had said that it was too bad about all the walking they would have to do the next day. You silly son of a bitch, Beaupre thought, it is safer to walk than to fly, you are so damn young. "Big William has all the luck," said Anderson. "Yes," said Beaupre, "it will probably be hot tomorrow," and thought, all the luck, lucky old black man.

"Hey, Captain Beaupre," the Colonel called.

Beaupre went back into the room. The Colonel was alone there now.

"I figure you to lose," the Colonel eyed Beaupre closely, "eight pounds tomorrow. Maybe nine. No eight. Five to the heat, and three for Dang."

Beaupre started to leave. "You want to stay with him. You don't have to, you know," the Colonel said. "It's an easy switch."

"I'll stay with him," Beaupre said. He answered almost without thinking; he did not know he had given that answer. High among the list of things he wanted to do was to get away from Dang. But he was aware how much pleasure it would give Dang if Beaupre were transferred and another American were assigned to him.

Beaupre left the briefing room and ambled back to the bar for his last drink. He was alone; Anderson had already gone to bed; before operations Anderson never had more than two cans of beer and always got plenty of sleep. Beaupre tore the chits out of his little book, paid for two brandies, and poured them himself. An officer was trustworthy, particularly when dealing with other officers' liquor. He cursed Vietnam and My Tho and the imposed celibacy on the uncelibate. The Seminary was fine for priests, they wanted it that way; if you want a seminary why not locate it at My Tho, no temptations here. The trouble was, it wasn't fine for grown men and particularly grown men who were going to risk their necks the next day. He remembered coming to My Tho the first day, trying to arrive in clean starched khakis, but waiting too long at Tan Son Nhut in the sun, and arriving inevitably wrinkled. He was greeted by a young and very handsome major.

"Welcome to My Tho, Captain Booprat."

"Bopray. Thanks. Good to be here."

"Sorry. Welcome anyway. It's not bad duty here."

"Why, doesn't look so special. Just a first glance."

"It's near Saigon, that's why."

"What about the local action. Any local sin?"

"None. They forgot to invent it."

"Local ladies?"

"Off limits to me. Off limits to you. Off limits to all long noses. Colonel's orders. Feels strongly about it—says it's bad for relations with the friendlies. You got something you have to do, you do it in Saigon. Big city. Two million people. Lots of ladies. Less chance of screwing your counterpart's cousin. Colonel wouldn't like that. Like I say, welcome."

"Colonel tightass, huh?"

"Nobody's tightass here, Captain, we all do what we have to do, and we don't always like it, which means that we do it a little better than we intended. Colonel's better than most. Doesn't have us whitewashing the coal bins if that's what you mean."

He took his second brandy and carefully considered whether he should shave now, before he went to bed, or try and cram it in the next morning, or finally whether he should skip it entirely. It was the kind of decision he took seriously because it was one of the few decisions which still had an element of privacy and personal control: if he shaved now, he would be, if not clean shaven, at least somewhat shaven; in the tropics his beard would grow quickly but it would be somewhat pardonable at the start of the operation. Tomorrow morning would be a better time to shave but he would be too rushed. If he didn't shave at all he would look sloppy when he greeted Dang in the morning and he would look even nastier as the day went on. He did not want to shave and yet he did not want to greet Dang looking grisly. He cursed the Army for winning all the small points, even here where you had a war and death and you were supposed to be free of chicken shit, you found that the chicken shit was a part of you, they no longer inflicted it on you, instead you inflicted it on yourself. He went back to his bunk and got his razor.

It was midnight. He would have to be up at two-thirty. The advantage of the helicopter units, the one tempting part of the assignment, was that they had the luxury of sleeping until four, while the ground units had to get up earlier. Donovan, the intelligence man, was sure that the VC kept agents inside the Seminary simply to gauge what time they were getting up; if it were earlier than two-thirty, Donovan claimed the word would be sent to the furthermost reaches of the sector; it had made sense (someone asked Donovan who the agents were and he had said he didn't know; someone else had said if we don't know who, why don't we fire them all and then start with a fresh bunch. Donovan had said it didn't matter, the same ones would come back in the fresh bunch), and then someone, one of the new lieutenants, had suggested they fox the VC by getting up even earlier on the days of operations; the Colonel had said he wanted to think about *that* idea, and mercifully it had died.

Beaupre if he were lucky might get two hours of sleep. He looked over and saw Anderson asleep, and then tried to fall asleep himself.

Chapter Two

BEAUPRE WOKE UP slowly and reluctantly from a
troubled sleep; for a moment he wished he had
not even gone to bed. He was dehydrated from
too much whiskey and brandy the night before.
He was annoyed by the number of mosquitoes
inside his netting and remembered that they had
woken him up once, or perhaps even twice; you
put the netting up and it kept out the air and let
in the mosquitoes. They rested now in the top
corners of the netting above him, but he could
hear them. He looked at one, and reached over
and grabbed it. He watched his own blood squirt
out. The mosquitoes were big and drank a good
deal, but they were also slow and easy to kill.

He shuffled off to the giant communal bath-
room (he had wondered before, not being a Catholic, if it hadn't been embarrassing for the young
priests; he had always assumed that priests were
shy people, how could they stand to start the day
with so little privacy). He managed in spite of his
own distaste to drink a glass of water; above the
long line of sinks was a huge sign which said:
"U.S. Army Medical Service Corps welcomes you

to My Tho. You may drink the water here, courtesy of us." The water tasted foul, thanks to the water purification man. The Army wanted to save his kidneys and his liver. He drank it anyway but his mouth cursed his kidneys.

At breakfast he drank two glasses of tomato juice, covetously eyed a third, and at the last minute his discipline held him back. He wished he had waited and skipped the damn water and held out for the tomato juice.

The eggs were cold and gummy and the coffee was the color of Scotch whiskey and tasted like the water purification man had washed in it. He tried to eat the eggs, and managed half his plate. He was still eating when the deputy division adviser came through, table by table, voice low, saying, "Five minutes more. Charley's waiting. Move it on, five minutes more, move it on and out. Hurry it up men. Charley won't wait. Hurry it up." Just as he finished the eggs, Anderson came by and sat down with his coffee. As they were talking, Beaupre looked at the huge pitcher of tomato juice and then poured himself another glass, almost defiantly, in case Anderson said anything about the heat. It was the first victory of the day for his real enemy, the heat. His uniform, as he walked out of the mess hall, was already stained under the armpits. It would be a long day.

At first he had despised the heat, but now he feared it; he envied the younger men who seemed to sweat so little, and he envied the older ones like himself, who seemed to have come to a truce with the heat, who could bear the worst of a bad day, and then say yes, it had been hot, as if that were that. He had sensed when he first arrived that the heat was the enemy of all white men, but it was more an enemy of his, he had less resistance and resilience; the others he sensed somehow managed to bounce back. His first day in My Tho had been an Easter Sunday, and there had been a major operation. It had been 100 degrees that day (he remembered the temperature of that particular day which was unusual, for like the others in My Tho he soon came to accept the daily weather as hot, and the exact temperature was never known: simply it had been hot yesterday, it was hot today, would be hot tomorrow, no one cared, one simply accepted it). It had been dry and there had been a long walk. Four Americans had been carried in with heat exhaustion. He had suffered at the command post, more mentally than physically, his imagination turning Vietnam into 365 days of this; when they brought back the second American, a young lieutenant, he began to feel giddy and appeared ready to pass out; this amused the then chief adviser who suggested that he take the Lieutenant's unit; then as Beaupre was getting his gear together, the Colonel stopped him and told him to take it easy, that it was a bad day. Later he learned that the Vietnamese thought it was a bad day too, and in the late afternoon when he helped take a lister bag of water to the troops he had found the Viets sprawled out, unconscious as though they had been drugged. He had loaded six of them into the helicopter and carried them back. The touch of their almost lifeless bodies had made him feel better, but he had known, too, that there were two enemies in the war.

He and Anderson walked out of the Seminary to a jeep which was waiting to take them to the

Vietnamese base, on the other side of town. A young corporal, one of the communications people, Beaupre thought, drove them over there. They were in the jeep a minute when he turned to Anderson and said: "You know what day this is?" Anderson said he did not. "Twenty-one days," answered the Corporal, "Three weeks is all. Exactly twenty-one days to go in this country. Then home, the land of the Big PX." Anderson nodded. "You mind if I ask you something, Lieutenant? How many days you got left?"

Anderson smiled, almost shyly, Beaupre thought. "One hundred and eighty-two."

"One hundred and eighty-two, boy, that's the best," said the Corporal, "downhill now. One hundred and eighty-three behind you, that's the important part, and nothing but downhill. Man, I remember when I got that one hundred and eighty-third." He turned to Beaupre and asked: "How many you got, Captain? You mind if I ask?"

"I don't know," Beaupre said.

"Whadya mean, you don't know," the soldier said. "Sure you know. Everybody knows. Even the Colonel knows. How many?"

"One hundred and eleven," Beaupre said.

"You sure about that, Captain?" the soldier said. "You want to be sure on something like that. I figured it out. Five hundred and four hours. Thirty-two thousand two hundred and forty minutes. You want to be sure." Beaupre said he was sure.

The soldier asked Beaupre when he got there, and Beaupre told him. "No," said the Corporal. "No sir, that ain't right. Can't be hundred and eleven. What day'd you come, sir?"

Beaupre told him.

"No sir," the Corporal said, "you don't have that at all. You got fifty-nine, maybe sixty days, no more."

"Sixty," said Beaupre.

"You ought to keep track of that, Captain," the boy said, "that's nothing to make mistakes with. They might leave you in this place a second time. You can't trust 'em. Got to do your own counting. They won't help you, not on something like that. Guess it's a good thing I happened to drive you this morning, otherwise you'd still be thinking you had four more months. Sixty days," he said, "that's one thousand, four hundred and forty."

"What?" Beaupre asked.

"Hours," he said.

"Thanks," Beaupre said.

They drove in silence, the sky still dark, the jeep lights on at half power, the air already a little heavy. Then Beaupre asked Anderson, "How many villages we got today?"

"Three," said Anderson, "Ap Vinh Long, Ap Thanh, and Ap Binh Duong."

"Ap what?" Beaupre said.

Anderson repeated the names.

"Haven't we been there before?" Beaupre said.

"Which one?" Anderson asked.

"All of them," Beaupre said.

"No," Anderson said, "none of them. All new objectives."

Beaupre thought for a moment. "You know what the trouble with this country is, Anderson? Too many villages. Too many goddamn villages, hundreds of them, thousands of them, all alike, and too many people in all of them. If there weren't so many so far apart, there wouldn't be any war, and there wouldn't be all this walking. Just take the people, and put them in one big city, get them out of the villages, and there wouldn't be any war, and no walking. And then you get those U.S. Aid boys, you know the ones with the fifteen-thousand-dollar salaries and expenses, and get them to invent a big machine which will plant the rice, and piss on the rice and kick the water buffaloes in the ass, and then pick the rice, and send it up to the people in the one city to count and eat, and you wouldn't have a war, and no Americans. We'd give them these machines free."

Anderson laughed.

"Some country," Beaupre said, "all these god-damn villages, all with the same name, apvin-hthanhbinhdinhlongdong."

They drove through the city now, the early risers beginning to wake and go to work in the markets, the people whose world in every country was always different from Beaupre's; they were always going to sleep when he was beginning to drink; being around when they were starting their day usually made him uneasy, but not here, not in this country.

"You know what that bastard Dang is going to say when he sees us this morning?" Beaupre asked.

Anderson began to laugh.

"He is going to say, 'ah good morning my friends the American warriors, ah good morning to you.'"

Anderson laughed aloud now, knowing Beaupre was right.

The jeep took them to a long line of trucks where the Vietnamese troops were waiting. The troops were already seated in the trucks, facing the wrong way so that they could not respond in case of an ambush. They met Dang, who smiled enthusiastically at them, patted Beaupre on the back and said, "My favorite American warriors. Ah good morning. Ah good morning to my friend Captain Beaupre and my young friend Lieutenant Anderson."

"Captain Dang, my favorite Vietnamese warrior," Beaupre said, and he thought he heard Anderson stifle a laugh.

"The Captain Beaupre is in a good humor today, and so is his friend Captain Dang. Today we chase the Communist Vietcong. I think we will do very well today and we will kill many Communist Vietcong."

Beaupre, diplomat, nodded and agreed and inquired about Mrs. Dang and the little Dangs.

"We'll kick the VCs' Communist asses, Captain Dang," Anderson said.

"Ah, the Americans," said Dang, "an enthusiastic people. Warriors."

Beaupre stood idly talking to Dang, thought that Dang was his reward: he had won him as at a raffle after his second week in Vietnam when he still had a certain element of drive and ambition. He had been assigned temporarily to another battalion, warned that the battalion commander was weak, warned also to behave himself, to be tactful, to be diplomatic, never to force his ally to lose face; that had been his first lecture, and he had nodded almost rhythmically as it had been given, knowing the words before they were spoken, knowing that he could roll with it and bend with it, he was an old pro. Ten days later they were on an operation and forty minutes short of linking up with the other units, when there was an ambush of the east force; the ambush had come at a time when Beaupre's unit happened to be taking a break, one of its many, they were after all spotted through the days like radio commercials. When he had heard of the ambush on the radio, he had noticed that the troops were still resting; he waited a few moments then tried to get the officer to move the unit. The officer nodded, agreed, but there were no new orders; the scene was repeated once more, several minutes later, Beaupre's voice hearing an added urgency, those were, after all, buddies ahead (he still thought of them as buddies then); and there was more agreement and still no orders, and finally two minutes on the nose, he had clocked it with his United States army watch, he had come back, angry now, this was after all one of the few things he found distasteful, leaving your own men open and under fire, shouting goddamn get them moving, move their asses, kick them, if you can't I will, move them, Christ, there're men dying now in these goddamn paddies, move them, your own people dying, what the hell kind of people are you. It had been an amazing scene which the Vietnamese troops had enjoyed immensely, smiling and laughing, and soon moving out smartly but to arrive too late; there had been a terrific stink afterward, and normally Beaupre would have been in trouble, perhaps his last march, but fortunately for him his predecessors had logged many long and similar complaints against the officer; the Colonel had made a stand and, small miracle, the Vietnamese backed down (the division commander had liked the commander of the ambushed battalion better than he had liked Beaupre's officer) and changed officers. The Americans were overwhelmed with excitement and pleasure, the new era, it was said, Beaupre was taken aside and told that it was a great victory but that he must not push it, he must above all things get on well with his new counterpart, he must get on, there could be no second switch, and no second incident, no more shouting about kicking asses, not even whispering about it (the Colonel had smiled when he came to this part). He must get along, he must bend, he must listen, advise and be polite; he had achieved a great victory and they were all proud of him, it was the Vietnamese who had been transferred, not Beaupre, but it could not be repeated; he had nodded through all this, surprised and a little proud of himself. Then he had drawn Dang as a successor. A week later he was asked about Dang, and he had said, and that was all he had said for a month, well he speaks better English than most; it was the first and last words of praise he had for Dang.

He talked with Dang while the young Vietnamese lieutenant who was Anderson's counterpart came up and started talking with Anderson; they seemed at ease, speaking first in English, and then as they walked away together, changing to Vietnamese; they seemed to Beaupre to be normal and young, and, for a moment, he envied them speaking Vietnamese and envied them speaking English, envied them being friends, envied them being young.

He turned back to Dang and they talked again, each telling the other that it would be hot, very hot that day.

They got in a jeep with Dang and went to the head of the file, and suddenly the trucks were on the road and the Americans in the jeep were leading the convoy; if there were a mine, they would touch it off. Along the road there were the stirrings of the coming day, the highway markets were being set up, and the children were already selling the cut sticks of pineapple. They stopped at a bridge, and what seemed like hundreds of children poured out from one little stand, waving pineapple sticks. The troops began to bargain, and laugh and shout at the children, one saying that he would buy the pineapple stick and the boy's sister for five piastres. They bought a lot of pineapple and Beaupre looked at it for a moment, lush and thick, translated its price to American currency, two cents, and then his discipline held him, but in the process he thought of the heat.

Then they were past the bridge, and down the sideroad, and soon they stopped, and left the trucks; and even that little strip of civilization, small as it was, the civilization of bareass boys selling pineapple, was behind them, and they were in the interior.

They moved out in single file. They were little men in big helmets, carrying big weapons. Curiously, the first time Beaupre had seen them in action, coming in on a helicopter, he had been surprised how big they seemed; he had expected them to be some sort of miniature soldiers, armed Boy Scouts, but from above it had been difficult to tell them from the American advisers until the last minute except for the difference in the way they walked— the Vietnamese had clearly not seen as many westerns as the Americans. But on the ground they looked small again, with the helmets mocking them and the war, neither soldiers nor Boy Scouts; somehow because of the helmets, it was not serious; the Colonel sometimes referred to them absentmindedly as "the kids." It was a beefed-up unit of the Eleventh Regiment, really a headquarters company plus another company, not a full battalion, and it seemed somehow, 150 men, more like a company than a battalion.

He watched while Dang talked to the Vietnamese Lieutanant, and then Dang said something to the troops, and they began to move, cheerfully.

He fell in at first behind Dang, determined, as he was most mornings, to try and start right, to try and work with his counterpart, an ambition which usually faded by midmorning.

"You think we'll have any action today, Captain?" he asked.

"Ah action," Dang said, "yes."

They walked side by side for several minutes and Beaupre tried to start other conversations; at times he had felt Dang spoke good English, but at times it was like this, Dang's way of isolating him from the unit. He had to go through Dang, he could not talk to the troops directly because of the language problem, and he sensed that Dang was pleased by this, that Dang was very sensitive to any direct contact with the troops; thus, given only Dang to talk to and more than 100 little men who smiled every time they saw him, he often did not feel so much like an adviser but rather a tourist in a foreign country. He was on a tour and he simply had more guides than most tourists; he could see it but he could not really touch it. At first this feeling had bothered him, he worried if

he alone were the outsider; then he had noted
that most of his American colleagues carried cameras with them, simple Japanese cameras which
they used to record Buddhist temples, dead
Vietcong, Vietnamese friends, and then one pose,
shot by a friend, of them with the old blackteeth
woman.

He looked at the troops: they had begun the
day wrong by sitting in the trucks so that they
could not respond to the ambush; he was sure
that most of their weapons were filthy (Beaupre
prided himself that he was not a great man for
chicken shit, but in a combat situation he believed
in clean weapons, and weapons that were always
checked). Now they were making too much noise,
they were always making too much noise. He did
not share the affection of most of his colleagues
for the Vietnamese troops. The other Americans,
he thought, were always babbling self-consciously
about how good the Viets were, how well they
behaved in spite of mediocre officers. But Beaupre
disliked them, he thought they made too much
noise, did not take care of their weapons and,
worse, did not take care of their buddies (though
their buddies, of course, would not take care of
them). It was reciprocal.

He had, he thought, behaved well: he had never
really had a fight with Dang, barely the hint of an
argument, and he had never lost his temper at
Dang. He had learned over a period of time not
to ask for too much, to ask for little and of course
get less; not to make too many suggestions, so that
first Dang would lose face for not having thought
of these things or done them earlier, and then he

Beaupre would lose face because they were not to be carried out.

They had been going for about thirty minutes when he decided that the time had come to make the first pitch. He was always careful: when he had an idea he did not simply voice it, but he thought about it, weighed it, and then decided whether or not it was worth making. They had been bunched up from the beginning, but he had held back, not wanting to begin the day with the most basic, most insulting, of requests, not wanting to use up what little credit he had. God only knew, perhaps just by chance there might be something serious later in the day, and there was no sense in being a smart-ass American right at the start. But they *were* bunched up and he *was* being employed by the United States' taxpayers for the specific purpose of keeping them unbunched, that was his salary, though it was little enough. One grenade, his first sergeant in Korea, an old and stolid man named Schauss, had said repeatedly, one grenade will get fifty assholes, if you keep bunching up: me Sergeant Schauss, I throw that goddamn grenade.

Beaupre halted and moved back to talk with Dang. The Captain smiled; he always smiled even when Beaupre was sure he was furious; Beaupre caught himself smiling; maybe, he thought, Dang thinks Americans are always smiling, even when they are pissed, smiling even when they ask the impossible.

Dai wee, he began, it was the Vietnamese word for Captain, and one of the few Vietnamese words he knew; so he used it a great deal, almost as a ritual; it was somehow supposed to say that he,

Beaupre, liked his, Dang's, country and people. The word embodied his sense of futility about the country. One of the reasons that Beaupre disliked Anderson, besides his youth, his eagerness, the fact that he would make captain in two years and major shortly after, was the fact that the Lieutenant spoke the language well, and knew, or claimed to know, what the Vietnamese were saying and thinking, spent more time with them and was able to laugh with them, even with the troops.

Dai wee, he began, and then speaking his own language, so much for international brotherhood, and speaking now almost apologetically, as if it were his, Beaupre's, fault that the troops were jammed up: "The troops are very close to each other." He smiled. The Captain smiled.

"Yes," he said.

"Perhaps," Beaupre said, "it would be better if they spread out a little. They are asking for the ambush."

The Captain nodded, and said something in Vietnamese. The word was passed back. Nothing will happen, Beaupre thought. There was an appearance of something happening; for a few minutes there was some juggling in the line, some rearranging. But within minutes they were all jammed again, ready for First Sergeant Schauss and his one grenade.

Beaupre moved up to the front of the line. He did not like being around Dang in general, and because Dang was next to the radio man, the VC often directed their first burst of fire there, hoping to get an officer and a radio man. There was no sense in giving them an American as well.

Besides, he liked being the point, or next to the point if possible.

By eight o'clock it was hot. He had judged his enemy correctly. When he had first arrived, he had set out to discipline himself. One canteen of water a day. The first sip after eleven in the morning. Not half finished before three in the afternoon which was the break-even point of the day, the cresting of the sun. No local fruit before noon. He had been very frightened by the heat and because of his fear, very determined. The rules had been very strict. Within two weeks he had begun to cheat; he had proved more human than frightened; within two weeks too much of his war was fighting the sun instead of the enemy, walking along dry rice paddies in the sun, and thinking not of where the enemy was, but whether he could hold out on water, where the next water was. At first he had cheated, saying to himself that his own discipline would improve, it was only a matter of time, a little longer in the country, and he would conquer the heat, he would become leaner and tougher, he would be in better shape. The miracle was not forthcoming: he was too old for this country; he did not bounce back. He had not changed or become leaner; he had remained the same and sometimes he had gained weight. On bad days, his uniform stained dark in his own sweat, long operations and strong suns, he would lose as much as ten pounds, but then there were always two or three days between operations and he would drink it back, in the morning, lunch, evening and bar (the Colonel, who knew what happens when a man starts to slip and was gentle, claimed tht it was the orange juice and tomato juice which did it, told him the bar was all right, but to skip breakfast). When he realized that he was not winning his war, he had begun to cheat, drinking from the canteen a little earlier, and then earlier than that, hoping that some fruit would appear early enough in the day, or that there would be some other benefactor, a chance and generous helicopter pilot arriving with a full and cold canteen. So far his luck had been good; only once had there been any real trouble, and then at the last minute, when he had feared that he must finally go to Anderson and ask for a drink of water, humble himself for water, the troops had found a coconut grove. He had sat there and sucked in the sweet juice, letting it splash over his face and neck, most of it running down his uniform, while Anderson had fumed because the troops would not move; Beaupre had been tolerant of the Viets that day.

With him at the point were two Vietnamese; he recognized one, a short squat man with a mustache, a Nung tribesman he had heard, who Anderson claimed was the best NCO in the company, and another slim Viet, one of the hundred. The three of them alternated moving in front; one would take the lead for a brief time, and then if it looked tricky ahead, one would take up a position of covering fire, another would flank the main path. They kept changing, and not a word was spoken; they could not speak English, he could not speak Vietnamese, but in this, if nothing else, sheer soldiering paid off, and there was no need to talk; instinct carried them.

They were joined after a while by the young Vietnamese lieutenant who nodded to Beaupre.

He became part of their ballet for a few minutes, and then as if by signal, he and Beaupre dropped back.

"The Captain seems to worry about the way the soldiers march," the Lieutenant said.

"Doesn't bother you?" Beaupre said.

"They are very close together," he said, "it is true."

"Why don't you do something about it?" Beaupre said.

"Does the Captain see generals' stars on my shirt?" he asked.

"They're your people," Beaupre said. "I don't have to write letters to their widows."

"We do not have the luxury of writing letters, in Vietnam," he said. "That is your luxury."

"They are your people," Beaupre repeated.

"So are the Vietcong," said Thuong.

Beaupre wanted to answer him, to say that the Vietcong did not bunch up, did not need advisers, but he restrained himself. As if by signal, the Lieutenant walked away and worked back in the file. Beaupre, angry, found himself thirsty; he was tempted to drink right then, but he decided he would hold, he would wait until after the first village. They should be entering the first village soon, within the half hour if they moved well, if they didn't pause too often for refreshment, and he would drink afterward. He hoped to leave the second village, just before noon, with a canteen half full of water.

Thuong dropped back from the point angry at the American captain and angry at himself. On the way he tried to break up the tightness of the formation.

"Stay away from each other," he said, "don't be so close. Would you walk like that if you knew the Vietcong were two hundred yards away? They are only going to shoot at privates today. No officers. Only privates."

He was in a very bad mood, and he was suffering considerable pain; he sensed that it was going to rain soon, and that would make his day even more difficult, his footing, already tough, would be more difficult. It was his day for stupidity; he had been walking for only ten minutes when he had felt his foot slip and sink into the hole, he knew even as he felt the foot descend and before the pain reached him what had happened; he had done this before, when he was younger and his clumsiness would have been more understandable. He felt the stake jab sharply and deeply into him and felt almost immediately the terrible pain in the fleshy part of his foot. He had said nothing. For an instant he was off stride, and the soldier behind him went on past, but another stopped to look and then realized what had happened to the Lieutenant. The soldier was about to move or to say something, but he happened to look into his officer's face and saw Thuong's stony look, which told him to move on, and the soldier, startled by the ferocity of that look, had not only obeyed but had seemed to leap ahead. Thuong would show no pain, he wanted no one to know; stepping on a punji stick he felt was something recruits and Americans did; the recruits were slapped in the face for doing it, and the Americans gave themselves medals, the heart of purple for doing it. He could have called a halt, even a temporary one, buh he did not. He did not want his own men to see it, and he did not want the Americans to see his mistake and to know that he could have made it.

He had knelt down, and quickly disengaged himself. He had felt the spike slip through the rubber of his boot, a military tennis shoe really, the pain worse as it was going out, and then a sudden flash of additional pain, so that for a moment he thought that part of the spike had stayed inside. He was almost sure of this because five years ago when he was a young and foolish aspirant, part of the spike had stayed inside him; it had been taken out weeks later from a green and swelling and evil-looking foot, only because he had been operated on, and then only because he was about to become an officer; the doctor, a Frenchman who had operated on him and had saved his life, had told him, in a very matter of fact manner, that had he been an enlisted man, he would certainly have died "comme tous les autres." The doctor then had given him a cigarette, pointing out that it was rare since he rarely gave cigarettes to the ones who were going to live.

He was sure this spike was infected, probably with buffalo turds, a VC favorite, they came cheap after all, and the more subtle forms of chemical warfare were not so readily available. He did not want to stop and clean it. He put his foot down and felt the pain stab back, and he knew that later in the day it would be very bad, and probably the next day even worse. He stepped ahead, carefully, and found that he could walk without a noticeable limp. He looked back and saw there was not even a dab of blood where he had stepped. He walked on the balls of both feet so there would not be a limp. He did not want the Americans to see him limp, to send a helicopter for him (it was their way of giving chewing gum to officers) or even to argue about sending a helicopter for him; it was, after all, an evacuation he could always prevent. He could keep going all day today and if he were lucky they would not spend the night in the field; it appeared to be a daytime operation only, so that he would be back in My Tho that night and he would be able to use some of his own piastres and send Dinh, the orderly, out for raw alcohol, failing that the local brandy which was raw alcohol with color, to dress the foot, and then hopefully see the doctor before the week was up. The alcohol would probably save the foot, but he was sure the money would end up with the Communists.

Behind him now as he moved back from the point he heard the troops talking and laughing. One of them was playing a transistor radio and singing along with it; a song about a girl who was rich and loved a boy, but the boy was poor, and so the boy, who was honorable, refused to love her in return, and so, of course, it was the girl who was forced to commit suicide; he wondered whether the song wasn't suspiciously like Communist propaganda.

"Binh," he said to the soldier, "do you know any rich girls?"

"Yes, Lieutenant," the soldier said. "A soldier has many rich girlfriends."

"They fall in love with you?" he said.

"Oh yes, certainly, Lieutenant, it is natural of them."

"But you did not marry them."

"I would not want to marry them, that would be

wrong, my obligation is to be poor. If I were rich, I would find it hard to defend my country and I would be tempted not to serve my country."

"So you would force them to commit suicide."

"Only to protect my country, my Lieutenant," he said.

"Perhaps you would protect your country by not walking so close to Private Thanh ahead of you."

"Ah, Lieutenant, then I was not thinking of protecting my country, I was thinking only of protecting Private Thanh."

Thuong watched while the two of them skirmished, Binh pushing Thanh and making him walk ahead, jabbing Thanh in the ass; the talk had given Thuong a respite, but only a brief one, and as he continued to walk back, he felt the pain coming at him; he was sure he was showing the limp, and the thought of that, and the giggling it would cause the troops, made him angry. He thought he saw one of the privates staring at him, looked at the soldier, saw the soldier staring back. He pulled the private out of line and demanded to see his cartridge case; the man produced a full one. Thuong was almost disappointed; with any real luck, the case would have been half full and he could have barked out an order, and thereby eased the pain and humiliation.

"Where is your medical kit?" he demanded, and the soldier, surprised by the anger in his officer, normally so calm, looked up at Thuong guilelessly and said he had none. The face was one of great innocence, and Thuong was about to give a rebuke, sharp and commanding, when he stopped himself and told the soldier to bring one the next time, you can never tell when you will be wounded or injured (or, he thought, put your stupid foot in a punji trap). The soldier smiled back at him and Thuong, in spite of himself, smiled.

"What great wisdom," he asked the soldier, "decided you to bring all your ammunition with you today? Did your wife check her horoscope?"

"I am simply a fortunate man," the soldier said.

"Do you know your horoscope?" Thuong asked.

"My wife says that her horoscope says that a very great man will be good to me this week," the soldier said.

"Your wife has a fine horoscope," Thuong said, "but what happened to it the day she married you?"

At eight-thirty they entered the first village. As they walked in, there was a report that two old men had been seen running out of the village on the north side. A squad was sent after them, but it appeared in no hurry moving out. Anderson told himself it was just two more old men who would never be seen again; but for a moment he was pleased by even this little flurry of events; perhaps, he thought, there might be some action after all. They moved toward the village, and he scanned the tree line and picked out what he thought was the best position for the Vietcong, a clump of bushes and trees to his right which had a commanding view of the open field in front of the village where the troops were crossing. He steadied his Armalite, and started to cover the position; he was aware as always that if the Vietcong were there, they would have an excellent view of him; because of his height he was the most obvious target. Were the roles reversed, he knew he would be distracted by any Vietcong who towered over the others.

They were not there. They entered the village without a shot.

Beaupre walked a few feet away and Anderson watched him; Beaupre appeared to be studying the entrance to one of the huts, but Anderson could tell that he was eyeing the giant cistern of rain water outside the hut. He is trying to decide whether or not to drink some, or put some in his canteen, Anderson thought. It might be poisoned, and at the least, it would require halazone tablets, which both of them detested. He's crazy, Anderson thought, he drinks all that whiskey and worse, and then he comes out here every day to die a little. Anderson watched the instant of indecision in Beaupre's eyes as he decided against it, and for a moment, he liked the Captain, and felt a rare touch of sympathy for him; for the moment Beaupre was not the cynical and bitter older man, but simply a thirsty soldier. I wonder, he thought, how he'll hold out the next time.

"Hot day," Beaupre said, walking back toward Anderson. Then he pointed to the Vietnamese, "Here they come with the mother corps right now."

The troops were assembling the women in the center of the village. There were about half a dozen women, and about four children trailing after them; in this village even the children had fled. The women all looked old, in their fifties and sixties, and when Anderson had first come to Vietnam, he had believed that they were that old. Thuong had taught him the truth, that some of these women were no more than thirty-five, but the life and the work and the disease and the bearing of children, live children and dead children, had aged them and robbed them of their sex. Their teeth had turned into the terrible mocking of the betel nut teeth, like black halloween pumpkins, their breasts so long departed as if never to have existed; their skin was not yellow, not brown, he could not describe the color, the color was dry, their skin was something you could strike matches on. Once when he was new in the country, he had said something to Thuong about understanding the country. If you want to understand this country, Thuong had answered, you should go to Saigon and the newest bar there, and find the prettiest Vietnamese prostitute and then take her with you, only you must not take her to a hotel, you must take her to her own home, in Cholon or wherever she lives, and you must sleep with her in her own little hut and listen to her mother and her grandmother spend the entire evening coughing into the night. Then you will understand my country.

One of the women was standing aside from the others and Anderson walked over and began to speak to her in Vietnamese. He said he was sorry if they had interrupted any work that morning.

He could see the woman's teeth: they were set and unyielding. He gave her a tentative smile. She did not reply.

He asked her if she were cooking something; if so, what. She did not even look away. He did not exist for her.

He felt a hand on his shoulder. It was Thuong. Without words he asked Anderson to leave the interrogation to Vietnamese. Anderson slipped away and went over to the hut where Beaupre was leaning. He thought he detected a very small smile on Beaupre's face.

Anderson felt slightly embarrassed, he was proud, after all, of his linguistic ability. He told Beaupre it was better if the Vietnamese did it.

The mocking left Beaupre's face. He was absolutely deadpan. "Maybe they were scared by your teeth," he said.

Anderson thought: you son of a bitch, I hope it gets even hotter today, even if I have to walk in it too. "You're getting to be more like them all the time," he said instead, "even beginning to think like them."

Thuong took over the interrogation reluctantly. It was, he thought, the part of the operation he disliked the most and as such it mirrored the change in his career. When he had first begun, as a young aspirant, he had liked this the best, and, he felt, perhaps because his parents were poorer than the parents of the other officers, that he did it better than the others, that he was able to play the role of the good officer. But each year it had gotten a little worse; the distaste had begun two years before when they had moved through a village they knew to be Vietcong and had found nothing; they were about to leave when a little boy, perhaps three years old, looked at him and began to weep and then ran to a tree by the canal and pulled out his father, a young Vietcong officer, a husky healthy young man. The father had never looked at Thuong, never said anything to him, simply walked to the child and began to pat him, to quiet him and keep him from crying; then finally when the child was silent, he had turned to Thuong and said, "Now which way do you want me to walk, north or south? Let's get on with it." After that, the war had gotten steadily a little older and uglier; they had, both sides, taken a higher price of these people, and the people had withdrawn into themselves, until it was more and more of a charade, more and more futile, more and more words on their part, fewer words on the part of the people, until finally it was the part of the war he liked the least. He sensed the political officers for the Vietcong must be experiencing the same thing, but they, he was sure, would have some phrase, some idea, some revolutionary rationale with which to continue, some fortuitous quotation from Ho which they memorized, and worse, believed. They would be told that it was for the people's own good, even if the people did not understand it, until perhaps in exhaustion and desperation the people would come to believe it too. Perhaps in desperation, the people told them yes, we promise to believe if you will promise not to come back here.

So now he began, wondering if his own feelings were showing: trying both to comfort and frighten at the same time, probably, he sensed, failing at both. He began with the question of the crop: did it look like a good one, he hoped so. He heard her noncommittal answer: didn't the Lieutenant have eyes, couldn't he see for himself, he was an educated man, perhaps he would look and tell her, a good crop and a bad crop, she could not tell the difference, they would be poor either way. He heard himself saying that they were luckier in this part of the Delta, that if they were living further south, as he had, near the U Minh (he had worked hard at it, losing his northern accent, and had been assured that it was gone now) the land was swampland and the children were not healthy. He looked down at the little boy beside her, and saw himself viewed with fierce anger, a boy four years old already knew anger and hate. He heard her answer that she was glad the military gentleman thought they were lucky. They had been unsure themselves. Only a wise and educated man would know something like that, she said.

He looked at the little boy, surprised and at first irritated by his hostility, then finally admiring the defiance: he would want his own boy to behave like this; then he noted the dark stain around the boy's crotch. He was surprised and admired the boy even more.

"Why do you come here?" he heard her say.

"Not because we want to," he answered. "Even for a foolish man like myself there are other things to do."

"This is not your village," she said. "There is nothing here for you, there is no money, there are no rich people here. If the people were rich, why would they want to live here?"

"We don't come for money," he said.

"We will be poorer when you leave," she said. "We always are."

"And when the Vietcong come," he said, "will you be poorer then too?"

"There is nothing here for them," she said, "nothing for you, nothing for them. We are poor even without you, without your help."

He looked at her and thought somehow (did one plant his own ideas on someone else, did he do this too often) she was not saying what she thought (Why are you one of them? What do you get out of it? Once his father, whom he loved, had said to him, Have they given you your American motorcar yet? and he had answered that unlike his wealthy father, he did not even own a motorbike).

"Is there anyone in the village who is sick and needs medicine," he asked, "the young children?"

"They will not take your medicine," she said. "As far as you are concerned, there is no sickness here."

"I have three children," he lied. "I would deny them many things because of my pride. But the one thing I would never deny them is medicine. If the Vietcong came and visited my family and left medicine, I would tell my children to take it."

He looked at her straight in the eye.

"I am sure," she answered, "that your children will be healthy."

She turned from him.

He could have stayed there and fought with her but he was a realist, there was no point in it; in the end, he would be forced to argue, to become angry and finally to take her prisoner with them for the rest of the day, and he was not up to that. So she had won, and he turned away and walked toward Anderson, realizing that he had not only lost to the woman, again, but had probably hurt the young American, again; he had pushed the American away and he had still failed to succeed with the woman: you do all the right things, and still it makes no difference, he thought.

He went over to Anderson, which was something rare for him, usually he broke contact instead of initiating it, and shook his head. He spoke in Vietnamese, it was his way of apologizing: It is getting worse all the time.

"Have you been in this village before?" Anderson asked.

"No," said Thuong, "not this one, but all of them. Everywhere we go now, everyone is angrier." We are angrier, he thought, the enemy is angrier, and the people are angrier. It gets worse every day. The peasant woman lies to me, and we get to the next village and another woman will lie to me, and so we will get to the third village and by the time someone there begins to lie, then the nice Lieutenant Thuong, so *bien élevé*, at eight o'clock will lose his temper, and make a mistake, perhaps capture some farmer, and then a couple of weeks later someone else walks into the same village at eight o'clock in the morning, and wonders why everyone there is already angry and bitter. And tomorrow at eight o'clock, I will be angry at my first village. It is a happy circle.

Anderson was Thuong's sixth American, covering a period of three years. Six times he had given the same lessons, six times at the least he had repeated himself during that period. Normally he would have had only three, but there were constant problems; some were transferred, one couldn't stand him, and one couldn't stand the pressure and had gone slightly insane, beginning to complain that too much rice was served at the Seminary where, in fact, rice was never served. Thuong had watched them with a steadily decreasing sense of curiosity, and a mounting sense of disappointment; when they had first come, and he was younger, he had believed they would work and that *they could change what no one else could change;* they did not, after all, lose wars, that was well known in all the history books (even the French ones) and they were big and rich (much richer, he knew, than the French) and somehow they would bring the touch for this to Vietnam. He had watched as the Americans arrived, and he had waited patiently for them to change the country, but first nothing had happened, and then suddenly one day he had realized what was really happening, that instead of changing Vietnam, they were changing with it, and becoming part of it; until finally he was more aware of their frailties than he was of Vietnamese frailties (Vietnamese frailties he saw as human frailties, whereas American frailties, because they were different and foreign, were American ones; a drunken Vietnamese in My Tho on Saturday night was a drunk, but a drunken American was an American; a Vietnamese coward was a coward, but an American coward was an American). His first American had come as a disappointment, a big heavy-set man named Rainwater whom Thuong had disliked intensely at first, a man who drank heavily and smelled of whiskey in the morning, and who complained bitterly about the country and the lack of war (he was always saying, "Where the hell is this pissant war you people keep talking about, Thuong," pronouncing his name Tooong, like a long whistle, then adding, "How can I fight this pissant war when I cain't even find the goddamn thing?"); he spent a good deal of time complaining about Vietnamese women and comparing them unfavorably with the Japanese, largely it appeared because the Japanese whores could speak English where the whores in Vietnam still spoke French, something he had never learned to do. The whores, he said, called him something like "beaucoo kilo" which he demanded that Thuong translate for him, the translation amusing Rainwater greatly. He had spent much of his year counting the days left and often at lunch would give the days and hours remaining. He professed to be amazed by the fact that Thuong himself did not want to leave the country too, as soon as the war was over, if they could ever find it in order to put an end to it; then Rainwater would give the answer himself: "But you're one of these people yourself." At first Thuong had thought him a fool and a drunk, but later in the last months (and days and minutes), had come grudgingly to like him and enjoy Rainwater for his honesty and his anger, even the fact that he used the adjective "little" every time he described Vietnamese and told Thuong that the Vietnamese were the worst soldiers he had ever seen, worse even than the Italians ("If I was to advise you to invade any country," he had said, "it would be Italy, but that was before I come here, and now I ain't so sure"). By the time Rainwater left, they were good friends with a surprising amount of mutual respect, though it is true that with Rainwater the myth of the Americans was once and forever ended, and they were in the eyes of Thuong at the very least a fallible people. Thuong was no longer fooled by Rainwater, and his pleas for Thuong to defect because he was "too damn good for this war and this here country"; similarly Rainwater was not fooled by Thuong and once in final days in My Tho had turned to him and said: "Toong, you sure are a funny little bastard. Thing about you is that you could be on either side. You don't give a damn for none of it, do you?" Rainwater, now out of the army at the army's request, was the sole American who corresponded with Thuong; Thuong's name was always spelled correctly on the envelope but inside the letters began faithfully, "Dear Mr. Toong." They told of the difficulties of selling used cars in Arkansas ("all the people here have been out of the Army for a long time and because of that, have become rich and therefore buy themselves only new and not used cars"); of Rainwater's troubles with his wife ("that woman is no good which I always knew, but now she drinks more whiskey than I do, which is bad"); of his apprehension on the increase in the pace of the war ("I hear you can find that little war now. Don't be no fool and get yourself shot and killed or even wounded because you ain't visited Rainwater yet like you promised"). Thuong often had difficulty reading Rainwater's handwriting in English and needed the assistance of Rainwater's successors who complied, though obviously disapproving of the contents, grammar, and spelling. The other Americans were to a man better looking soldiers than Rainwater; there were, as the war continued and the war became more important in America, more of them, and they were younger, better educated, slimmer and more sober. Instead of counting the number of days left, they were often threatening to reenlist; they were earnest, always careful to praise the country and its people, never used the word "little" as an adjective in describing Vietnamese, and never referred to the Vietnamese soldiers as

Rainwater had done, as our Gooks (to him the Vietcong had been their Gooks). But to Thuong they remained a disappointment; they were brave, professional, and competent, but they were curiously without passion. Thuong saw them as actors rather than soldiers: they came full of idealism, they tried, and then they accepted until soon they mirrored the same frustrations and fatalism that he saw in the young Vietnamese, indeed, the same frustrations and fatalism he saw in himself.

There was little they could teach him about the war, little they could teach him about frustration, or about how men react in combat and how they look when they die. When they did have valid points on things that could be changed, even under Captain Dang, he accepted these in somewhat bad grace, so that he knew (there was after all a playback among the Vietnamese about what the Americans felt) that he was regarded by the Americans as an arrogant little bastard but a good officer, "the prince" in fact had once been his code name. Of all the Americans he was quite sure that Anderson was the best officer he had seen; brave, intelligent, handling himself well with the Vietnamese soldiers, speaking the language better than any American he had ever seen; similarly he was sure that Beaupre was the worst, sloppy, careless, indifferent to the troops, contemptuous of the Vietnamese, and worse, he was sure he sensed Beaupre's fear.

They stayed in the village for fifteen minutes. While they were there, the American radio came on and said that Beaupre was wanted. The Captain went over to Anderson's radio.

"How's it there, old buddy," the CP said.

"It's quiet here," Beaupre said, "except for the noise we're making."

"Quiet on the eastern front too," said the CP, laughing at his own joke.

"Any prisoners there?" Beaupre said.

"No," said the CP, "you got any?"

"Just Anderson and me," he said.

"Pretty good," the CP said.

"I'll talk to you later. You be careful, hear. The Colonel says the time to worry is when it's quietest."

"Thank the Colonel for me," Beaupre said.

They got ready to leave the village; soon, Beaupre thought, I can have some water.

Anderson got up ahead of him, walking up and down the troop file, checking the troops out.

He heard a cluster of Vietnamese troops giggling, and he looked over in time to hear one say, or he thought he heard one say, the American is looking to see if we have taken any chickens. He heard them giggling. They were right, of course; it was exactly what he did.

"No," he said, "I was checking to see if you had taken any of the women with you, or if any of you had stayed behind to protect the village."

As they moved out of the village Anderson could feel the difference in their pace; he sensed the letdown, if anything, they were going slower than usual. He decided to prod them and push them a little harder.

He worked his way to the front of the column: faster, he told the Viets, faster now, the faster we go, the quicker we get to the rice. They laughed and he asked one of them if he would share some rice with a poor American; they laughed again and for a moment he liked the country and the

. assignment again. When he had first arrived, he had tried hard to talk to the troops; encouraged at first by their easy humor and their easy response to his kidding, he had tried even harder and had asked more serious questions only to see them somehow float away and become uneasy, their eyes gaze off; when they answered, there was a quality of apology as if somehow they felt they were disappointing him by telling how poor and simple their lives really were. Why would anyone want to know these things: they were born, they grew up, they went into the army, they died; they apologized for the telling, and turned away, embarrassed to be taking his time even to repeat what was so obvious, to give foolish answers to foolish questions. He had also sensed that if the conversations were too long, Thuong would be uneasy. So Anderson had continued to get on well with the troops, but it had been a limited affair, built on his promises to swap their rice for his Coca-Cola (sometimes they insisted that he eat their rice, which he did, reluctantly, since it was dotted with black spots which he could never identify and made him constantly uneasy but which he bravely swallowed; he had little confidence in their field hygiene).

Move on, he was saying now, you people are as slow as American troops, move on, move on. How are we going to march to Hanoi if you walk like that. How am I going to meet any Tonkinese girls if we go this slow. Come on, there won't be any hotel rooms left in Hanoi and the Rangers will beat us there. You don't want the Rangers to get to the women before you do. Move it on.

They delighted in this and he was relatively

sure they were laughing at what he said and not at his language construction: he had checked these phrases out very carefully with the full-time Vietnamese interpreters at the Seminary so that there wouldn't be any grammatical problems.

"Move it on," he said, "speed it up, or we'll never get back to My Tho, and you'll have to go three days on that rice. You move it on, now, or I'll never get back to America and never see my wife, and she'll have to marry some general."

He had wanted to make some remarks about their own women, suggesting that civilians and garrison soldiers would be in their beds unless they hauled ass, but he was not sure that a Westerner should say something like that to a Vietnamese, perhaps it would be considered racial or insulting, coming from a foreigner, and so it was only his own bed which was threatened; he had tried the other line on the interpreters at the Seminary and they had laughed, and said, oh, yes, that was fine and funny and the troops would like that (the interpreters looked down on the troops and thought they would enjoy any joke which mocked them) but he had decided against it. So now he pushed and prodded and talked about their rice and not their women.

He kept pushing until he came to the point where he found Beaupre. They walked side by side for a while.

"Anderson," said Beaupre, "you think we're going to see any lovin' Vietcongs today?"

"Your friend Captain Dang told me we were going to kill beaucoup of them," said Anderson. "I believe your counterpart. What he says, we do."

"My friend, the warrior, Captain Dang," Beaupre said.

"You wouldn't want me to doubt your counterpart."

"The goddamn Communists are too smart to go out today. They'll wait till it's cooler. Yes sir, they'll sit today and drink their rice wine, with their lady Communists, and they'll take it easy. They got the radio network which is reporting how many clicks we walk, and how much we're sweating, and they get the news and they laugh, and the lady Congs pour them another rice wine, and if there's no more in the bottle, they send the lady Congs out to the PX for more and they laugh a little more at us, and they wait till it's cooler and then they knock off a VC piece. You think I'm kidding, but you ever seen a Vietcong sweat?"

Anderson, appreciative of this Beaupre, laughed; the man was a study in torture, his uniform black, the sweat rolling down his face, but at least he was joking.

"You know why we're here, don't you?"

"To kill beaucoup Congs, like all good American warriors."

"No, no, that's the cover. We'll kill those VC, mind you, but the real reason is to visit his kinfolks here. You see the wife of Captain Dang is from here, originally, and they would put up a plaque to her saying how she married the Captain, except the Vietcong would pull it down. But Madame Dang's kinfolk is everywhere here, and you see his wife is married to the province chief's sister, whose nephew married the cousin of the district chief right here in this very district, this very district, mind you, where the uncle of that cousin was once the head of the village, the village in this district, only Captain Dang has forgot which village it is, so we are visiting all three villages and maybe more, and hoping to find the right one, and the right village chief, it's a homecoming."

Beaupre seemed to want to continue; and Anderson thought, he is talking out his thirst; he must be nervous, perhaps his thirst is nervous. But out of the corner of his eye, he saw Thuong moving up and he was sensitive about Americans talking too much to Americans; he knew that Beaupre had made his distaste for the Vietnamese clear to Thuong, and he did not want to be identified with the Captain.

Anderson was a chosen young man: a West Point graduate, but not too high in his class so that he would spend the rest of his career frightening superior officers, rather a well-trained young professional, with the right attitudes, and tastes, and a carefully muffled ambition. He had completed the Ranger and Airborne training, had been with the best line units in West Germany, married a German wife, volunteered for Vietnam and had learned Vietnamese. He had come with high expectations to Vietnam, and had been disappointed since arrival: disappointed with the war, the Vietnamese themselves, with the Colonel, and disappointed with Beaupre.

He had not taken Beaupre seriously at the very beginning: they had met the first day at the Seminary, Beaupre back from an operation drenched with sweat, undressing and holding up each garment so his bunkmates could see how it had been soaked through (T-shirt, skivvies, socks, everything), a scene which had shocked Anderson—it had seemed, at the least, unmilitary, unofficer. They had gone out on the first operation together, and Anderson, who had volunteered for Vietnam, assumed that everyone else did too; he had asked Beaupre why he had come to Vietnam, and Beaupre had thought for a minute and then said with great honesty, "To get away from my wife," and from then on they had never really communicated well. Now, sometimes Anderson felt that if perhaps he had paid more attention to Beaupre, shown him more respect, asked him more questions at the very beginning, they might have become better friends. But he had instinctively shied away from Beaupre and his table, with the sense of a young man who is going places and does not want to be with men who are not going along, whom he knows will not be promoted, will never, he was sure, make major, who sit each day and complain about the country and the war; they were not his people and he was not going to share their defeat. Later, when it became clear that they were going to spend most of their time together in Vietnam ("You have been given the assignment," Beaupre said, "that countless young girls in Seoul, Saigon, Paris, and many other places where we have fought and died, are seeking, the right to spend the night in the open skies with me"), it was too late to reverse the snub which had come at the very beginning when, instead of eating at Beaupre's regular table at the mess hall, which was if nothing else, a combat table—Beaupre, Raulston, and others like that—a sour combat table, he had chosen to eat with younger officers, all of them rather like him, "the caydets," Raulston called them; Raulston made a point of saying that he was not, as he put it, an Annapolis man. Later when Anderson realized that his assignment made him more nearly a member of the Beaupre-Raulston table (the other young officers were in signals and administration and jobs like that, not combat men), it was too late; if he had shunned them because he distrusted their lack of ambition, they in turn distrusted him for his youth, his ambition, and the fact that he did not complain about the country, the army, the war, and the food. (Raulston was bitter over the food. He claimed that Vietnamese shrimp were the best in the world, but the mess hall would not serve them because they were unsanitary; "everything in this whole goddamn country is unsanitary, but the shrimps are the only unsanitary thing that taste any goddamn good. I say we give up chipped beef because it is a known, proven, researched medical fact that chipped beef is unhealthy and unsanitary in a hot climate, and that we keep the shrimp instead; if I get hepatitis, I goddamn well want shrimp hepatitis and not S.O.S. hepatitis.") But Anderson tried to bridge the gap and from time to time would talk to Beaupre about the country, about the differences between Vietnamese from the southern and Vietnamese from the central region, and the Captain would say: all island people are like that; Anderson would say: what island? and Beaupre would say: *this island,* of course; and Anderson would be troubled and bothered by the conversation, not knowing whether Beaupre was serious or kidding, and finally letting it go, but a week later he had quietly started the conversation on the subject of islands and island people, and finally had become more specific, and Beaupre had said: "What island, I've never been on any island; what the hell are you talking about, is that what they teach you at West Point?" It became a pattern: if the Lieutenant claimed that the Vietnamese were brave, Beaupre might discuss their cowardice, telling tale after tale of how they fled from battle; if Anderson insinuated (after all, he was too good an officer to do more than that) that the Vietnamese were not quite so brave as he had expected, Beaupre might answer with a long and detailed account of Vietnamese heroism, once telling how he, Beaupre, had been carried off the battlefield by Viets (a story spiked by Raulston when questioned by an uneasy Anderson: "it'd take fifteen goddamn Viets to carry that lardass off, and besides if it was that bad, he wouldn't wait, he'd get his tail off quicker than they could unless the VC had already amputated his legs for him. Besides which, he ain't shy about being a hero and he ain't told anyone here").

Anderson shuttled back and forth in the line now. They moved so slowly, always so slowly. He wanted to yell at them, to push them, to pick them up and carry them. Instead he coaxed them and teased them; he knew it was an impossible task but he continued, not so much any more to change them, he knew it couldn't be done, not today anyway, but because he had learned early in his tour that unless he did this and burned up his own energy, their slow pace with their short legs and what were for him mincing little steps would exhaust him, the act of holding back more exhausting than the act of letting go; the talking and the shuffling were an outlet for his own energy.

He wanted to yell at them, to pick them up, to court martial them, anything, but he said instead, "Move it on, if you go that slowly, I'll never get back to America, I'll never see my wife again, I'll spend the rest of my life in My Tho, and I'll have to join the Vietnamese Army, and I'll have to marry a Vietnamese girl. Move it on, help me out." It became like a song.

This was one reason why he liked the helicopter assaults: there was in that instant of debarking, the roar of the engine, the fear of getting hit in the head by the whirling rotor blades, and getting hit by the VC, a drive that carried you further; he sensed that the Vietnamese were aware of it, that when he had heliborne units, they went a little harder and a little faster; he thought they really loved the helicopters, it was as if that made them like American soldiers, lofted around in and out of the sky by American pilots it became, he thought, a booster shot of pride as if they themselves finally believed they were real soldiers.

He was still annoyed about not getting the helicopter assault; so much of the country and the war had disappointed him, so many other aspects of the country had let him down, that this had become increasingly important; it was the part of the war which pleased him the most and the part which had become the most valuable. In six months when he went home, he wanted to be a specialist in heliborne assault so that he could be a member of the brand new Airmobile Division, an entire division with nothing but helicopters (which was training, according to Beaupre, to come right the hell back to Vietnam); it would be tough to be a member of that division, but if he made enough heliborne assaults, he was sure it would show in his record: it would salvage Vietnam for him.

Vietnam had begun well for him. He had wanted to come to the country, had volunteered for it, had wanted to do it properly so that he had even given up the chance to come in one of the first batches and had stayed behind for language training. When he finally arrived, he was ready to fall in love with the country and the people: indeed, even as they had flown over the rice fields on the way in, he had been awed by how green the color of the country was, and deeply moved, he had thought: this country is in Technicolor. He had never forgotten how green it looked and that sense of life which it had seemed to reflect, it was a giant garden. At the airport he had been pleased by the little girls, so slim and polite, in their native dresses, so oriental. He had been delighted when he spoke to them and they spoke right back, the people, he thought, are not too shy. The first night he had left the other Americans at the hotel barracks in Saigon, broiling thick American steaks on top of the hotel on American charcoal and drinking American beer; Saigon soldiers, he had thought, and had gone off to a Chinese restaurant alone. On the way back he had taken a cyclo deliberately instead of a pedicab or the prehistoric bus which the Americans were supposed to use and which was recommended for officers (with its grill wire over the windows to stop terrorist grenades; terrorists, it was said, preferred officers); he had been excited as the cyclo rushed through the zoo of Saigon traffic, inches away from collision after collision with bikes laden with fruit, men with crated live ducks, children, even goats, he thought. It was night, and with the air cooler there seemed to be more excitement, more energy, and he wanted to yell out, mix his sweat with their sweat, his joy with their joy (he assumed it was joy); finally it took control of him and he did yell, a long, happy whoop, scaring the cyclo driver who stopped the cyclo and waited to be chewed out for a wrong turn; but no attack was forthcoming, it was, the driver decided, just one more drunk American. The next time Anderson let go with a whoop, the driver whooped too, and soon they were playing a game: Anderson whooping, then the driver whooping; the driver whooping, and then Anderson returning the whoop; Anderson finally giving him the largest tip in his history.

The second day in Saigon had not been so pleasant. He had started off intending to make a complete sight-seeing tour of the city and had even given the cab driver a list of the places he wanted to see, carefully marked out in Vietnamese. The cab driver had looked at them, had smiled at him, and had begun to drive; they were in the cab about two minutes when the driver had turned around, smiled rather broadly, and said, "Jiggedy jigg jigg." Anderson had not understood and had looked puzzled and had answered in Vietnamese; the cab driver turned again, more insistent this time, a touch of a leer, and said, "Jiggedy jigg, jigg." Anderson did not understand the words— after all, he thought the cab driver was speaking Vietnamese, and the cab driver thought he was speaking English—but Anderson understood the leer, leers after all are not just oriental, they are international; but by the time he understood it, the driver was more insistent: "Jiggedy jigg, jigg, numbar wan gull," with three gold teeth, Anderson would remember those gold teeth a long time. Finally, in desperation, Anderson stopped the cab, threw one hundred piastres at the driver, and walked back to the BOQ, disliking Saigon all the way.

Vietnam had troubled him with consistent regularity ever since; he had been pleased with the assignment to My Tho, that was where the action was; indeed, if he were a man easily embarrassed, he might be embarrassed by the letters he had written his wife in the first month ("they are a shy and sensitive people," he had written, "and one must be always interested and trying to make an effort. And always formal. They like formality. It's part of their tradition and their culture. Some of the guys here get pretty chummy with their counterparts, and slap them on the back, but I don't think that goes over so very big. I think the better class of oriental people resent it"). At the beginning he had sometimes sensed the possibility of really contributing: he had had two of his suggestions accepted by his first counterpart, one a prize for the soldier with the cleanest rifle, a weekend trip to Saigon, was discontinued when the first recipient extended the weekend to three months. He had sensed a breakthrough at the beginning and had talked excitedly about this with the Deputy Division Adviser, a disappointed older man about to go home to retirement, who had waited through Anderson's enthusiastic discussion and then had said only, "Watch out for these goddamn people." Anderson had not paid much attention to the Colonel and indeed he had thought of writing to his wife and telling her that he might reup for a second tour. He decided not to bring the subject up at the time; nevertheless, his letters continued to report on the gentleness of the people, the good humor of the soldiers, the charm of the children, children everywhere barefoot, bareass, laughing, begging for candy, grinning and even shouting out newly acquired American curses; in all, he was taken by what he decided was the purity of the country despite all the death and suffering. This sense had come to him one day early in his tour; it was in the second month and they had walked through most of Dinh Thuong province, mile after mile, with Beaupre complaining bitterly, "Jesus Christ, we have walked so far we must be in Cambodia. You speak any Cambodian, Anderson, you ask the next peasant how far to Phnom Penh." But Anderson had not minded, he was still able to learn about the country, still reveled in the greenness, and he was charmed by the peasants shepherding thousands of baby ducks from one bog to another.

On that hot day even his sweat felt good, clean and healthy. They had passed through three villages and were on their way to a fourth and were just outside it when Anderson saw some movement at a distance, a file of men, he decided; it couldn't be VC, he was sure of that, the VC would not move in such a tight file. He decided it must be Civil Guard but then as the file drew closer, he saw that they were not soldiers at all, not even men, they were young women astonishingly young and pretty, all dressed up in their *ao dais* in so many colors that for a moment the file looked like a moving rainbow. Then the two columns approached each other, only ten yards between them, the troops weighed down by their weapons, incredibly clumsy, and the girls dainty and graceful, no longer a rainbow, now a ballet troupe. He had a sense they were floating by. As they approached, Thuong shouted angrily at the troops telling them to keep their soldiers' mouths closed.

"What is it?" Anderson asked.

"A wedding," Thuong said. "We still have time for it here."

For a moment as the two columns passed each other silently, Anderson wanted Thuong to stop so they could pay their respects and tend their best wishes; he was touched by the moment and proud of it, this was why he was here. But Thuong seemed to sense his question and shook his head and they walked on. As the two lines passed, the girls did not look at the troops, their eyes fell to the ground, but later he heard a light chorus of giggles. But Anderson was moved by this, and for a time it symbolized the country for him, so that later he was able to remember the wedding party and forget the soldiers who were saying, behind him:

"There goes the last virgin in Vietnam."

"Ah, she will be thinking of you tonight, Phuong. You have just ruined her marriage."

"It is always the same."

The first month had been the high point of his tour, of seeing and touching and learning about the country. By the third month all real hope of a breakthrough was clearly ended; by this point he and Thuong were well into their long, difficult, almost torturous relationship, neither friend nor enemy, neither stranger nor confidant. The illusion of breakthrough was gone and Anderson was resigned to the frustrating daily task of being an adviser, of forgetting about big victories and trying to ward off big defeats. He reconciled himself to this surprisingly well; he looked for the positive side of the day and discounted the frustrations. Yet increasingly, he wondered whether he should have tried for Special Forces; there they had no trouble with the Vietnamese, they had all the money they wanted, and they ran the whole show. By the time he left for Vietnam, there was so much talk about Special Forces in the States that anyone not in the Army who heard of his assignment, automatically assumed that he was in Special Forces. His wife's letters indicated that the problem still existed; whenever her friends saw a television show on the Special Forces, they would call Mrs. Anderson and tell her to rush to the television because her husband might be on the show. Anderson was so enraged by this that he had written excessively detailed instructions on the mission and responsibilities of both advisers and Special Forces, letters sufficiently detailed to resemble field manuals, and noted that Special Forces came in twelve-man teams: "two officers, nine enlisted men, and one television cameraman." His wife, surprised by the intensity of these letters, faithfully reported it to her friends, who just as faithfully continued to call her whenever there was a television special on the Special Forces. Indeed, pinned up over Anderson's bunk was a long article from a major magazine about a Special Forces camp which had been overrun, quoting a lieutenant there as saying: "All I want now is the

Combat Infantryman's Badge" and underlined with Anderson's own comments: "Then come on down here to the Delta and earn it."

At times like this, he thought as he prodded the troops, he envied the Sneaky Petes, up there in the mountains where it was cool and with no Vietnamese, and with little montagnards who did whatever they ordered; he was not at all sure that they didn't have the best part of the war. It wasn't like that in the Delta, he thought: when they tell you about war, the one thing they never say is how slow it is.

Chapter Three

BEAUPRE WAS GLAD to leave the village; he was sure it belonged to the enemy and hated the folly of it all, sitting there having tea parties with the enemy, giving them medicine, being polite when they lied, smiling when they rubbed crap in our faces; all these villages were the same, with the same people, the same thin, mean, suspicious faces, the same lies and half lies; and every time they lied, he thought, we smile. They hate our goddamn guts, and they would as soon kill us as look at us; if Germans had looked at us like that in World War II, he thought, we would kill their asses right then and there; the Germans, he remembered, had been afraid to look at them like this. He remembered a Jewish platoon sergeant who, when he came to his first village in Germany, had assembled about ten villagers and had given them orders in Yiddish, telling them to smile, to stop smiling, to smile again, to frown, to cry, and to smile. Then when it was over the sergeant had walked away and had started to cry himself, weeping that we were all too soft, too nice, too gentle.

Side by side now he walked with Anderson after the village, still angry and uneasy.

"Goddamn, but I'm tired of getting crapped on in this country," Beaupre said. "They sit there and crap on us, and after we leave they sit back and laugh how they did it."

"You think you're any different from me," Anderson said. "You think we like it, any of the rest of us. You think the Vietnamese like it?"

"But they put up with it. They take it, and because they take it, we take it. And the more we take it, the more we get. These goddamn Vietcong see it. They see when we walk in that here's an outfit that takes crap, and so they give us more, and we take more, and we'll take more tomorrow; and the more we take, the more they hate us. No wonder we don't get any damn respect." Why here they come again, he thought bitterly, that nice government company; the one that took so much last time and they liked it so much, and now they're back for more, and they got that Beaupre with them. Sonny, go back in the hut and bring out that extra sack of it we've been saving.

"That's the name of the game, taking crap, being nice, being patient. That's why we're here, and that's what we're paid for, and it's my job and it's your job, and you're senior to me which means you get paid a little better for taking a little more of it."

"You still believe that," Beaupre said. "Don't you ever learn that the people who teach you that crap don't believe it, they're the last people to believe it. Don't you know that the officer who gave you the lecture on how not to screw Vietnamese women in small towns because it's bad for public relations, he's the first man to find himself a Vietnamese moose; that's why he was picked, because he's an authority on the way life really is, he's the only man back there who can give that particular lecture with a straight face. Haven't I taught you that if nothing else? Don't you know those people up in Saigon don't give a damn about winning friends, but it's their job to make you think it's important, and so they go ahead and they give those lessons."

"You'd be more of an authority on that subject than I would, Captain."

"You bet your goddamn ass. I'm more of an authority on that subject, on a lot of subjects, than you are."

"Sure you are, and you'd be tough. You wouldn't take any crap from them. You'd stand up to them, and if they didn't behave and show you the proper respect and smile, you'd take them back to My Tho, and you'd make Vietcong out of every single one of them, Captain. But you'd be tough."

"You can't make Vietcong out of them. They're already Vietcong and they were Vietcong back when you were still in West Point, Lieutenant. They've been what they are a lot longer than you've been what you are." Some war, he thought, smile at all the peasants, be good, be nice. The Ipana War. What did you do in that Vietnam war? Killed three VC, and kissed 346 peasants.

They separated, each of them angry at the other and angry at themselves for this burst of feeling. It was unusual; they had never been friends, there were too many differences in background and style for that, but there had been some mutual respect and most of their anger and their hostility and their difference in philosophy had been kept in the background. Occasionally it would come to the fore, but rarely with such feeling as now, and they both regarded it as a mistake and they were embarrassed by it. There were enough real enemies in this country without fighting each other. So instinctively they moved away from each other to cool down.

Beaupre walked ahead, relieved now. If nothing else, he could have his first drink; he had, he realized, teased himself with the water; he had passed the first discipline of the day, and now each minute was an additional victory. But his thirst was terrible and he felt the power of the heat. So far his legs were responding well and were not wobbly. But it was as if he were surrounded and enclosed by the heat, a prisoner of it. The sweat rolled off his face and he could stick his tongue out and taste it; the sweat was in his eyes, and he felt under his hat, his hair soaked through (he was losing his hair, and he was convinced that because of Vietnam it was falling out even quicker, that enclosed under his hat there was a sort of Turkish bath taking place and his hair was being driven out). The stains under his armpits were gone; simply the rest of his uniform had caught up with the stains, from a distance his uniform looked just slightly darker than all the others. In the process he had started with the stain under his armpits, then a stain on the backside of his ass, then a stain at his knees, and then a stain around the rim of his hat, until finally his whole uniform was soaked. He looked at his watch and wondered whether he could hold out for ten minutes more. He tried, looking at the Viets, and saw that only a few of them were touched by light dabs of sweat. He made it for six more minutes, and then took his canteen, opened it and drank. He was surprised by the desperation with which he took the water, and then to his shock, by how much he had taken. When he restored the canteen, it was much much lighter.

He checked his watch and realized it was time to check in with the CP. He sought Anderson, who carried the radio and told him to check with the CP (the Colonel had instituted the practice of American radios; most other advisory units depended on the Vietnamese radio communications but the Colonel wanted his own network; he knew the Vietnamese disliked it, but he thought it kept them more honest and kept them moving, and that it might save lives). Anderson got on the radio, and the CP came in very clear: no contact, east or north.

"What about the helicopters?" Anderson asked.

"Nothing there," the CP said. "It was a perfect landing, just perfect."

"Why so perfect?" Anderson said.

"Nothing there," the CP said. "Big William says it's a chopper pilot's holiday. All three lifts came in without a shot being fired. Another day, another piastre."

"If it was so goddamn perfect, where are all the VC?"

"Just a long hot walk in the sun," the Lieutenant said. It was one of his favorite phrases. Beaupre nodded; so his fear had been wasted: he had been frightened of the helicopters because he had studied the war, and studied in particular its death, and had finally decided that the most dangerous part was the heliborne assault when you landed in the open and they might be dug in and ready. The advisory staff had not lost many men, but most of them, he was sure, without an exact count, had been in circumstances like that. He believed if you walked in, with company- or battalion-size units, the chances of death were slimmer, much slimmer. So this time he had been too smart. Now his unit would have to walk longer and further on the ground than the heliborne units, which not only meant a longer battle with the other enemy, the sun, but also that the factor of death was now against his unit instead of the Rangers because the heliborne unit was larger and therefore less likely to be hit.

Anderson, he noticed, seemed happier with the news. He had missed nothing, after all, had not been cheated. He had missed a drama and then had found it had not taken place.

"More goose eggs," said Anderson. He was not yet cynical about death, but he no longer was fooled by these operations, and sometimes Beaupre sensed that he might come to like Anderson yet, perhaps by the end of the tour. Perhaps if his wife wasn't so blonde and pretty and tanned, and if there were one photograph of her instead of three, if she didn't write the Lieutenant twice a day, perhaps if she didn't, as the Lieutenant kept confiding to Beaupre, keep writing, saying she hoped he would return so she could be pregnant and have twins. In contrast there was no photograph over his own bureau and there were almost never any letters for him. He did not really know about his marriage. It was not very good, and he did not like to think about it. When they had first asked him to come back to counter-guerrilla warfare, he had agreed, in part because of his marriage: perhaps the tour would save it or finish it, he had thought in a vague way at the time, although he was not sure which he really wanted. This war, which solved so little else, would not solve his marital problems either, he suspected.

"But you don't like the helicopters very much," Anderson said.

"No," said Beaupre, "no, I don't."

"How come?"

He wondered if he could tell him all; that it was not just helicopters, that it was everything new about this war; helicopters, spotter dogs which were guaranteed to find VC but were driven insane by the heat and bit Americans instead, water purification people, psywar people, civilians in military clothes, military in civilian clothes, words which said one thing and always meant another, all these things, and particularly helicopters, nowhere to hide in a helicopter, you try to get your ass down in a helicopter and it's still in the same place, exposed, worse, elevated for them, nowhere to run, nowhere to hide, all too modern for him.

"Because it was designed so they can see you better than you can see them. Check it out, you'll find it was Communists who invented the helicopter," he said.

He moved back toward the point and told Anderson to watch the tail part of the file. The heat had already begun to take its effect; it was not so much that his legs were tired, but that he was glad now that the Vietnamese went so slowly.

He wondered why he did this, why he went out on these operations. The Colonel, after all, had given him a way out; he was not going to be promoted, it would make no difference in what little was left of his career, and no difference either in what little there was of this war. He would not save the war, he had no illusions there; and he had been offered a gentle way out by the Colonel. He saw himself as a man without false pride, yet here he was walking where he didn't want to walk in a war he didn't want to fight; he cursed his foolishness and his pride which had brought him here—it was the kind of false pride he ascribed to people like Anderson. As he walked he thought of the Colonel's offer to pull him back; right now he could be back at the CP talking on the radio, giving off kindly assurances to angry men in the field—stay in there, don't sweat it, nobody here expects the impossible, arguing with the helicopter people, telling them how safe the LZs were, and all the time drinking great glasses of the iced tea the Colonel kept there (a practice started by his predecessor who had learned that when Saigon generals dropped in they always liked to have a glass to drink, and iced tea was better than water). He was, he knew, probably the most cynical of the officers in My Tho, and yet here he was, one of the handful walking through the operations, and probably the only one walking who would never get a promotion and who already had the combat infantry badge. He took another drink of water. He kept walking, and sweating, and he was just about to reach for the canteen again when they walked into the rain.

It happened quickly ahead of them, a thin sliver

of the horizon had suddenly become darker. Then minutes later they could see the land ahead of them, places where it was raining, and places where it was still sunny, and then suddenly it was pouring down rain, a rich tropical downpour, total rain, really, and they walked into it; even as they did, the rain seemed to reach out and move toward them. He walked in just as he might have walked into a shower. He could see about fifty yards to the left of him where it was not raining. He had done this, walked into rain showers like this many times before in Vietnam, and it had never ceased to awe him, and, indeed, there were moments like this when he wished he were a child so that the sense of awe could be even greater. He knew the particular agony which would surely follow: his uniform would be completely soaked with water, heavy with it, like a towel which has fallen into a bath, and then the sun would come out, stronger and more determined than ever, drying the rain off his uniform and giving him a terrible steam bath in the process; then probably more rain and more sun and steam, and so on. It was a form of torture which might be fashionable in some woman's beauty salon, but it would be agony here. Nonetheless, he would suffer it: joyously he cursed the rain. He continued to walk in the same manner, but he tilted his head up and opened his mouth to the rain, and the palms of his hands were, for a brief moment, extended open to the sky.

The rain had made the footing more difficult for Thuong; he was putting his weight forward and it was the kind of ground now where you should dig in the heels. The foot continued to bother him, but the pain for the moment was not as bad as he had feared; it would be worse the next day, and worse the day after that, he thought.

Behind him he could hear the troops laughing over the village: one was saying that the only Vietcong there were pregnant women, and the other answered that he had visited these villages so often that he was the father of five Vietcong soldiers, and then the laughter of several of the troops and finally the first soldier saying that when they entered the village, the women said: "Here comes the company with Private Thanh, the billy goat company." They all laughed.

The village had bothered Thuong while he was there, but curiously it was bothering him more now that he had left; there had been something there he hadn't found out, there was an attitude there that he had begun to sense only after leaving and which he hadn't picked up in time. It was not only that they were hostile, and even a bit contemptuous of him, but that they were almost too cool, too sure, as if they knew something that the Arvin didn't; it was as if his visit there had been expected, the interrogation had been expected, and they had even been able to rehearse their lines. Their reaction to him and to the troops had been too sure and certain.

He had not liked this operation from the start, not so much at first for what it was, but for what it might have been. He was tired of walking everywhere in the sector without finding the enemy, and without wanting to find the enemy, and this operation he was sure was designed to hide from the enemy while allegedly still seeking him. Captain Dinh, who was the intelligence officer, and one of the few staff officers that Thuong trusted, had reported a company moving southwest of My Tho and believed the company was pinpointed about fifteen kilometers south and that chances for contact were good. Dinh was a shy little man which explained why he was an intelligence officer, shifted there at a time when no one thought intelligence was important and when there was a certain quality of rejection and failure in being assigned to handle it. But Dinh himself had been relieved by the selection; he had confessed to Thuong of mortal terror at the possibility of being given troop command:

"Suppose I give them an order and they just don't do anything, they just stand there. I know it will happen, that they will look at me, and then do whatever they like. They are all older than me."

Freed from the nightmare of giving orders to hundreds of his countrymen who would then surely disobey them in unison, Dinh had applied himself diligently to the role of intelligence officer and had turned out to be very good, a success which proved to be somewhat annoying to many of his superiors. Thuong had enjoyed the inevitable scenes where Dinh, at first innocent and unknowing and indeed dangerously enthusiastic, would spout off his intelligence without realizing that no one wanted to hear it, that the more he talked, the less he was listened to, the silences which greeted him growing longer and more audible by the minute. Finally Dinh had learned some sophistication and was less enthusiastic, but he had a handful of good village informers, and he was stubbornly loyal to them; if they were going to take the risk of living in what was often alien territory, he, Dinh, was going to make sure they got a hearing in the great councils. Thuong found the byplay amusing; of all the men in My Tho who would never make major, Dinh was the leading candidate (besides himself). On this occasion he had rather quietly outlined his reports, though not with the rigid certainty he had shown a year ago. When he had finished, Colonel Co, the Division Commander, had praised him, and then outlined his own operation, known in the code book as Operation Happy Green Flower. Dinh was not enthusiastic about Happy Green Flower; it was, he told Thuong privately, something of a political operation planned long in advance, and settled perhaps ten days earlier; it had bothered him enough that the original intelligence was old and somewhat dubious, coming from sources he didn't entirely trust, and pumped up by the province chief who was a friend of Co's. There was something else a little troubling, he said; in the last twenty-four hours there had been a second wave of intelligence, fresh bits here and there, inklings from agents' reports, including agents he trusted, which indicated some sort of movement in the area; he was not sure what the movements were or what they meant, but he had duly reported it. Co, at first, had looked somewhat surprised and uneasy, but then had smiled broadly and had said that it showed that the province chief was certainly right and that Happy Green Flower would kill many Vietcong.

"I do not like your Green Flower," Dinh told Thuong later.

"Thank you, but it is your Green Flower," Thuong

said. "I only go where my intelligence officer wants me to go."

"Ah," said Dinh, "you are the most arrogant officer at My Tho, so arrogant that you allow yourself to be different from the others. They are simple men compared to you."

"I will ask Co for permission to take you along with us and put you in command of the troops," Thuong said.

Thuong was interrupted from these almost happy thoughts of Co planning an operation long in advance only to learn at the last minute that there might be Vietcong in the area (an angry Co, because to change at the last minute would lose him face with the Americans, the province chief and most of the staff officers), when the forward elements brought in a thin old man they said was moving south.

The old man immediately began to kneel and mumble something, and Thuong told him to stand up, for God's sake, he wasn't a priest and this wasn't confessional; but this only scared the peasant more, and he remained kneeling; Thuong repeated, for God's sake, stand up, no one's going to kill you, we're all too tired for that. Out of the corner of his eye, he saw the American Lieutenant approaching and he immediately waved the American away; at least the fat American, who was disagreeable and who cursed the Vietnamese in public, was bored by interrogations which he did not understand and did not like. Thuong smiled at Anderson, almost a wink, really, and said under his breath, why can't you be like your fat friend? He turned to the peasant and began the inevitable: you walk quickly for an old man, the old man

saying he was old and not important and if he did
not walk quickly he would be a poorer man. They
sparred some more, and the old man said he was
leaving because all the people from Ap Chinh Be
were leaving their village that day. No, it was not
his village (said with surprise, did he look like
someone from Ap Chinh Be?), it was the next
village, his village was larger. Had the Vietcong
come to his village? No, he was not a Vietcong.
Thuong said he was sure, but had the Vietcong
come to his village? No, they had not. Then why
had the people from Ap Chinh Be left the village?
Oh, he didn't know, that is another village, and
they do not talk to us, the people from that village
are very strange. You would not want to trust
people from that village? Thuong asked. Yes, that
was it (and a smile, impressed with the Lieutenant's knowledge of the two villages). No Vietcong
there? No, no Vietcong. We could put you at the
head of the column and let you test for us. You
are the officer.

Thuong wondered what small percentage of
the truth this old man was telling. Perhaps 20 per
cent, perhaps not even that. But in this country
what was the truth any more, could you find it,
and if you did, did it matter? You told the truth
and you were killed for it, you lied and hid the
truth and perhaps you survived; the truth was a
terrible luxury. A man wanted to live, that was the
truth and he would lie to do it; and anything he
said was designed not for honor but simply to
gain the next day. So there was the great truth, he
thought, living, more important than anything
else. So the old man was telling his truth, he had

seen no Vietcong, heard of none, would speak of none; perhaps he had told the same truth the night before when the Vietcong had arrived and he had said no, he had never seen a government agent, never paid them taxes, never heard of the government.

"Why do you tell me so many lies?" Thuong said to the old man. "Do you think I am stupid, do you think I am more stupid than you?"

He wondered what he could do; he could put the old man at the head of the column, or he could bind him up and trail him behind, or perhaps he could tie a rope around his neck and lead him along like a dog, the Vietcong did that with government officers and captured Americans, tied their hands behind their backs and put ropes around their necks and led them around for the villagers to see; but if you are going to do that, he thought a little bitterly, you need something more spectacular than this, this thirty kilos of peasant.

He signaled to one of the men and told him to let the peasant go. He knew it was the wrong thing, that by the rules he should have kept the man, and that he might get in trouble for it, but he felt tired; and he didn't feel up to the rules of the war, taking this old man and draining the truth out of him, crushing him until all that remained was the pulp of the man and a few drops of Thuong's fine truth. The old man knelt before him and began to talk and pray and thank Thuong all at once, and the Lieutenant, angrily now, shouted at the soldier, "Get him out of here. Out of here. Now!"

*　　*　　*

Five minutes after the prisoner was released, Dang arrived. Dang said he hoped the peasant had brought good news, news about the Vietcong.

"What kind of good news," Thuong asked (I *am* an arrogant bastard, he thought).

"That they are waiting and we will smash them," Dang said.

Thuong looked at him and wondered whether the man knew the difference any more when he was talking to Vietnamese or Americans: even when they were talking to other Vietnamese they were making speeches, he thought; they surround themselves with themselves; Colonel Co is surrounded by lots of little Cos, one of whom is Dang, and so he is making speeches to himself; and the Dangs in their turn surround themselves with younger and more subordinate Dangs, lieutenants, and make the same speeches, though perhaps somewhat more modest.

"What did he say?" Dang was repeating the question.

"He said he had never seen a Vietcong in his life, and that he did not trust the people in the next village."

"Was he a Communist?" Dang asked.

"Perhaps. He pretended to be afraid of us. I don't know. Perhaps he was. Perhaps he wasn't."

"You took him prisoner?" and Thuong shook his head; Dang knew damn well that the man had been released, it was all a game. And now Dang barked out angrily, why had this been done? A Communist who would report on them, where they were, how many weapons they had (and where, thought Thuong somewhat cheerfully, the company commander stood in the file).

"I didn't want to collect old men. If we took him prisoner, he would slow us down, and I thought he was too old to kill. And they probably know where we're going anyway. Three different government forces are moving toward one point. They would have to be stupid not to guess where we are going."

Dang was furious now. His voice was sharp and angry, and Thuong listened, almost amused by Dang's anger; he no longer minded provoking him. He heard the words pouring out, *insubordination, disregard for my men,* and he noticed how shiny Dang's face was, it glistened. He wondered whether Dang would change his place in the file now. He heard Dang promising to take over all interrogations. No more tea and medicine, Dang was saying.

Thuong let the Captain finish, and he wanted to say something arrogant, but all that came out was, I know you will do well, my Captain, and I thank you.

"Did you learn anything from the peasant, Captain Dang?" Beaupre asked a few minutes later.

"No," said Dang, "he was an old man on the way to the market so I let him go."

Anderson moved forward to see Beaupre a few minutes later to tell him what he sensed and half understood (he had watched the conversation between the two officers, and had watched Thuong's face, cool and almost happy, and Dang's obvious anger).

"Dang is most highly pissed off at Thuong over the prisoner," he said.

"Who's Thuong?" Beaupre said.

"The Vietnamese lieutenant," Anderson said.

"Oh, that one," Beaupre said, "the cocky one. Your counterpart."

"Someday," Beaupre told Anderson, "if we are lucky and brilliant and brave, we will capture an entire Vietcong headquarters, and we won't find any young men. No sir, we'll find nothing but thin old men and these old women. Nobody there under fifty. Then we'll find out that each day we've been releasing nothing but VC commanders and generals, that every time we find some raggedy ass peasant trying to repair a bike, why it was a VC general."

"You mean you think Dang is right?"

"That little prick is never right. He could end the war tomorrow or even better have me shipped home tomorrow and he'd still be wrong. All he wants is another goddamn statistic. He's probably pissed they didn't kill the poor bastard farmer. He'd even claim they captured a rifle."

"That lieutenant say anything back to Dang?" Beaupre asked.

Anderson shook his head.

"Too bad," Beaupre said, "the Lieutenant's a lot better than that bastard."

"What do you think?" Anderson asked.

"Shit, boy, you remember what I told you last week? That's what I think, I told you to buy that extra insurance, young hero."

So under that hot and relentless sun, they kept walking; the morning slipping back into the boredom which commanded so much of their time and their resources. The sun weighed on them; they did not talk to each other, there was nothing to say. Complaining about the heat would not solve it or drive it away, and the heat was too strong, it drove other thoughts out of their minds, until they continued on in an almost insane rote march, the time slow and heavy for them. Step followed step now, not because they thought of it, but because it was automatic, they did not even know they were walking.

The heat was there, nothing could be done about it. When Beaupre was new in the country, he had joined a group of advisers pressuring the Colonel to try a night operation; his motivation, however, had been largely different from that of the others. They were intense younger officers who argued that since the enemy always moved and fought at night, it was time to challenge him. For Beaupre all this made sense, but his thoughts were not of catching little VCs stamping around overconfidently in the night—not that, he thought of the cool of the night and moving around without dying so many hot deaths from the sun. So when the Colonel had asked his opinion, he had said yes, why not? The Colonel, good officer, had his doubts and kept saying things like, do you think they're really ready for it, bad thing if it backfired. But the young officers were sure of it, they had all talked with their counterparts and their counterparts all wanted it; everyone seemed to want it except the Colonel (which hardly explained why it had never been tried before), and so the Colonel finally surrendered and worked on Co, and Beaupre got his chance to walk in the cool of the evening. It turned out that the Colonel was right, they were not ready for it; it was a disaster; the darkness of the night only magnified all their flaws; battalions strayed from regiments, companies separated from battalions, platoons from companies. For days afterward soldiers straggled in; and the rate of defection was the highest ever. It was a terrible evening of units stomping around blindly in the pitch black, and one battalion adviser, new to the area, when asked where he was, answered that the sign said the village of Ap Chien Luoc; this was duly passed on to the Colonel, who having kept his calm through all these other failings, and sensing that when this disaster was reported to Saigon it would be his disaster and not that of the young officers, exploded and yelled to the radio man, *tell that silly sonofabitch that it's like being in the States and being in the village of Drive Carefully, every goddamn village here has a sign saying Ap Chien Luoc, it means strategic hamlet.* It was not a success from the Colonel's point of view, and it was not a success from Beaupre's either; the absence of the sun turned out to be too little reward, he was tired, he was eaten by endless mosquitoes, and he was in terrible fear of being shot from behind by accident, or of being shot by Raulston or someone else if they stumbled into another government unit; the night operation made the day a little more bearable.

He was not the only one who suffered from the heat. Anderson felt it too, but for Beaupre there was a quality of terror in the simple act of walking; he continued to sip from his canteen, drinking too frequently now, losing all sense of discipline, paying no attention to his own rules. The heat had finally begun to make him uneasy, not yet dizzy but no longer sure of himself, worried now about the outcome of the day. They came between villages to an intricate network of canals, and he began to feel some of the fatigue, his own reflection of the sun's power. There were no bridges over these little canals, simply thin little trees laid across, their surfaces slim and slippery; it was a part of the march that Beaupre always hated. The secret on the narrow bridges was to walk quickly and have your momentum carry you across, and if the canals were a little too wide for that, the Vietnamese would stick a pole into the canal midway alongside the one 'span and they would then use it as a cane support while crossing. Beaupre had always detested these bridges; he lacked the build to do them gracefully ("all you have to do, Captain," said the Colonel who had mocked him when he had first come to the country, "is think of yourself as a ballerina. If you think of it that way, you won't have any trouble"); and Beaupre had slipped and fallen in several times. It was humiliating and demeaning he had thought, even at the beginning, a man his age, straddling these damn things and trying to walk gracefully and then falling flat on his ass into the water in front of the giggling troops (the little bastards, he thought, had a lower center of gravity; they wouldn't laugh so much if they weren't so damn small). A man his age ought to be allowed to make a fool of himself, he had thought, but he ought to be able to choose the time and place and type of fool he wanted to be.

He had no trouble with the first of the three canals (as he passed over it he looked at the intricate network and thought what an ideal place for an ambush, a unit would be completely pinned down and would never be able to move across without exposing itself, soldier by soldier, dead soldier by dead soldier). But he was tired and on the second bridge he had made the terrible mistake of looking down and then thinking about the possibility of falling; he had looked at the water, dirty, murky, tepid, vile, how many people had pissed in it that day, and for a moment he had hesitated and almost slipped.

The third canal had been a little wider and he had been nervous by the time he started; on the bridge the Viets were going too slowly and had jammed up, and he had been forced to stop and wait and he had looked at the bridge, thin and slippery from the muck on their boots. He had stopped and thought for too long a moment, and when he finally started again, he did what he had almost willed himself, he started to fall, and he slipped off the bridge and into the water, slowly, so that by the time he hit, with his shoulder, he had one arm out to break the water, and another holding his weapon above his head. He went completely under, the water was warm and filthy, and though he tried to close his mouth, it was too late, and some of the water got in. He came up spitting and coughing and cursing the goddamn canals, and the goddamn bridges and the goddamn country (he rarely cursed himself) and the water. He was angry and soaked with the warm filth of the water; despite the heat, it was not even refreshing; he was angry and humiliated. He looked back to where the Viets were still standing on the bridge, but they were completely silent. He angrily pushed his way out of the water, climbed out of the canal, and began to march again, when he realized he had lost his pistol (not his really, Raulston's, they had swapped because Raulston had admired a Luger he kept; when Raulston had given him the Colt, there were only two bullets in the chamber; he had demanded four more, but Raulston said you only needed two, one for Charley and then one for yourself). So he walked back into the filthy water, hating it, he had never been in water so warm, and squatted down and started to grope for the pistol; he would not, he vowed, put his head under that water again. He could feel nothing but the muck on the bottom, when a Viet jumped off the bridge and looked at him for a sign of what was missing. Beaupre signaled a pistol, and the Viet stuck his head under water like a diver, and a moment later proudly came up with the pistol. Beaupre, more humiliated than ever, thanked the Viet clumsily, realizing he did not know the Vietnamese word for thank you. He started to reach in his pocket for some piastres, and then decided that would be the worst thing to do. He smiled at the soldier, and it was returned. He felt old and foolish. He walked on but in his walk there was less swagger. He let the sun steam the warm water out of his uniform. He was probably lucky, he admitted to himself, that he had missed the pistol so quickly; it would be difficult to describe to Raulston the loss of a pistol, and those two bullets. He never carried more.

He took his canteen and wasted precious water cleansing his mouth out; he was not even sure any more whether his mouth tasted foul; the impor-

tant thing was that he thought it did. He spat the
water out; his canteen was already dangerously
low, perhaps, from the feel and the angle of tilt,
one third filled. He wished now that he carried
two canteens of water. It was a logical enough
idea; the troops in the South Pacific had done it
during World War II, though they never knew
when they would be resupplied; but at the Seminary no one else did it, and so his false pride had
hurt him once again. It would be a simple thing to
do.

He made Anderson get the CP on the radio.
Everything was just fine, the CP said, just clock-
work, running off nice and smooth. No buggering
it up (when he said this, somehow Beaupre sensed
that he was saying there would be no buggering
up unless Dang and Beaupre buggered it up).

"What about Raulston?" he asked.

"Some old women got pissed off at the friendlies
for the usual and then attacked some of the troops,
and so Raulston decided he would play the big-
nose judge and make peace, and he like to have
lost both eyes from those women. Said he'd never
seen women so mad, made his own wife look like a
lady. He got pissed off himself and had three of
them taken in. Says he's never been so scared in
his life, kept shouting: 'I am your friend, I am
your friend, I am good American,' and they kept
coming. He left a message for you. Want it?"

Beaupre said yes.

"Raulston says it's pretty damn hot over in his
part of the country and wants to know how things
are with you. Says he made an arrangement with
the Colonel to fly home in the choppers if there's

an extra lift, and you can walk. Says you'll understand, the both of you bein' buddies and all."

"Tell him," Beaupre said, "that's fine, and for him to fly over us on the way back, so we can just signal them friendly like, just like buddies."

"Colonel asked about you, too," the CP said. "Wanted to know how you were holding out, and if everything was okay. I told him you were just fine, and plenty smartass, same as ever, but he seemed a little worried and he wants you to pass the word if the heat gets too much."

"Tell him no sweat. Heat's okay," Beaupre said, but later he wondered if he had said the right thing; whether it wouldn't be better to go in if there were a medevac chopper; and finally whether Anderson had said anything to the Colonel.

They walked along, and Beaupre watched the troops with a certain grudging awe; they were not bothered by the heat. It had taken no toll. Instead there was still a quality of an outing, he thought. The troops had their food with them and some of them were already nibbling from the hunks of cold rice glued into a lump. Others were gnawing on sugarcane stalks. Several times that day he had been offered sugarcane by the troops, but though he enjoyed sucking on the cane, it had become part of his own mythology that somehow sugarcane made him thirstier, like drinks of Coca-Cola; it was somehow too sweet.

After the first hour of the operation, if there were no contact the troops always relaxed; the rattling and babbling seemed to go up, the pace was slower, the background noise of giggling seemed to increase. Sometimes he was inclined to compare them with American troops and to be shocked by their lackadaisical and relaxed attitude in the face of combat situations; sometimes it seemed to him combat interrupted them only as rainstorms: they walked and joked, there would be a brief ambush, a few men killed, the ambush would end, and within minutes they would be walking again, laughing and talking again, imperturbable even with death; whatever their faults, and American troops had many, they would not be so casual with death. Then he would wonder about American troops if they had been going over the same ground in the same war for five years or more, and he was not so sure the Vietnamese were very different. Even with himself, there had been change: when he had first arrived, he had brought with him a sense of total tension and tautness fashioned out of World War II and Korea; he still remained, he thought, professional, but it was a more relaxed, more acclimated professionalism; he bent with the wind here, he did not go at 100 per cent capacity in a war which was fought at 5 per cent capacity; it was all very well to think as they suggested, no, demanded, at the indoctrination briefings—Vietcong to pop out from every single bush or jump up from every canal, or hide in every single hut ("Victor Charley is always where you don't think he is. Victor Charley is always outthinking you. You are sleeping and Victor Charley is thinking, planning, cleaning his weapon," they had said at that last briefing)—but if you thought like that, you would soon be exhausted. There were simply too many bushes, canals, huts in the country to fear and too few VC to hide there; one would have to be a raving maniac if he spent his first three operations chasing VC every-where; by the fourth he would be in a state of physical and mental exhaustion and, of course, Charley would step out and zap him. It was a lousy goddamn war. So he went at his own pace, with his own sloppiness; if you were to be ready in this war, you had to roll with it and feel its pace. The Lieutenant, Anderson, was different: Anderson was young and ambitious and hungry and there was no quality of relaxation to him. Each ambush was an enemy and a duty; each VC was a step toward promotion; each successful operation was a victory for his country, duty and honor and country and the Point. He had seen the Lieuten-ant before, often in Korea. In Korea it was almost as if they had been mass-produced: young, strong, absolutely fearless, they came there as if off a production line at home; they led, often a little too bravely, and they died; they went back almost as quickly; they died well, their troops mourned them (he never heard the troops in Korea who bitched frequently about everything else complain about these young officers; it was not just the West Pointers, it was all of them as if the ROTC men, in order to prove they were as good as the others, were trying to out-Point the Pointers). And so believing everything they were taught, they came a little too quickly, and died a little too quickly and were replaced a little too quickly by someone just like them, eager to take their place. He sometimes wanted to reach out and tell them that they had been badly briefed, that none of it was true, that it was the cautious ones who would live and survive, and make it home and give the briefings, and it is the cautious ones who get ahead. But those who survived would have to learn for themselves, or not learn for themselves. They would not, he knew, believe it from him: lessons on advancement in the Army were not something old captains were authorized to give; they would take those lessons only from someone who had gotten ahead.

For the first time that day Beaupre considered that it might be a reflection on him that he had not gotten the helicopter assignment. That was, after all, the elite assignment and demanded the best unit, the best coordination, the best American-Vietnamese relations, the best officers, the real tigers. He was not, after all, an American tiger (and when the Colonel teased him about Dang, was he not also teasing Beaupre about being Beaupre, saying in effect that Beaupre and Dang deserved each other, were well mated, that he had decided not to waste a good adviser on Dang).

Once he had been a tiger, a good killer, with a taut, if somewhat unwieldy, body; but he was overweight now and even when his uniforms were fresh, he managed to look just a little bit sloppy and wrinkled. Not all of this was his fault: he was too old and too fat for this war, and he had not wanted it, not sought it. He had been sitting in the United States completing faithfully, if listlessly, the final years of his twenty, filling in at those places where the United States Army had long ago, for reasons no one any longer remembered, assumed responsibilities but where it was not deemed wise to waste chosen young officers—one of his last posts had been as teacher at prep school ROTC courses. These were not posts he would have wanted; but for four more years the United States Government was permitted to be wiser than he, they owned that much of him. The ROTC assignment had not been unpleasant or taxing and indeed the principal difficulty had been in watching his language among the students. There had been one reprimand and two near reprimands, but not much was made of these lapses, since it was assumed by his superiors that this type of failing was organic within the Army; all the Beaupres before him (and all the Beaupres after him) had drawn roughly the same number of reprimands, it was a truism of the Army that anyone so ungraceful in career as to be assigned to that position would have a serious language problem. He had not minded the position; he had long since written off advancement, promotion and similar miracles, and he had been content to check on close order drill (generally performed with more enthusiasm at these schools than by real recruits in the Army) and daydream away on the possibility of affairs with the wives of some of the instructors, for there were favors hinted and certainly promised; but it had struck him that it was not a fair match, an irate husband with tenure at some little school would somehow frighten the Army, and it would be Beaupre who would be dispensed with. Besides, the women on the average weren't worth the risk. He had been performing his official functions and not performing the unofficial ones when Vietnam erupted again and when counter-guerrilla became the fashion. By chance someone, perhaps an IBM machine, turned up the fact that earlier in his career, he had been a line crosser in Korea (an IBM machine certainly would be ruthlessly

oblivious to the added weight and age and fear he
had acquired in the intervening time). He had
worked for a time filtering back and forth across
lines, working on prisoner-snatching, a job assigned
to him because when the call went out for volun-
teers his battalion commander had not liked him,
had viewed him as expendable, and had volunteered
him.

In 1961 they had called him and told him
rather pointedly that he was an expert in guerrilla
war; he had protested, he knew nothing about
guerrilla warfare, for a limited time he had done
a very limited type of operation, and he had been
luckier than most, he had survived. They had told
him that his modesty was becoming but that what
he had done qualified him as a guerrilla fighter,
he had been *behind enemy lines* and the fact that he
was still alive testified to the expert quality of his
work. Many good and glowing things, they discovered now, had been said about him at the time,
about his toughness, his ability to smell out traps
("sometimes I think Beaupre has a Korean nose,"
they read from an old report); they told him of
his valor and cunning; they seemed embarrassed
about the ROTC business, it was a mistake, a big
Army, Beaupre would understand, and thank Heav-
en, they said, it was now being rectified. He had
protested—though naïvely pleased about the report from Korea, which was true—but he had
pointed out that he was nine years younger then,
with less weight and more wind and motivation,
besides he was already involved in the ROTC
program. They needed him, they said, and ROTC
didn't, they made that clear; indeed, it would be
good for the ROTC program, they added, to be

able to say that Captain Beaupre had been pulled out in mid-term because he was needed in Vietnam, it would give the ROTC program more style, he could serve it better in Vietnam than he could there, it would be like lighting a candle for ROTC. He protested again but because they made it an order, and because he was bored with his wife, with his life, he accepted.

At the very first he had been asked to give a course at Fort Bragg on special warfare and infiltration. He had walked in the first day to lecture all the lean young men, and he had looked something like a gentle porcupine, roly-poly, and not one bit the infiltrator. He had sensed their amusement (all the other instructors were young embryonic Marlboro men); and so the next day he had come to class wearing *all* his ribbons and their amusement had ended, but perhaps he could mark it as the time when his own had begun. For he had never felt at ease: their questions were always too eager for his answers; they were sharp and alert, his answers were vague and uncertain; they saw his ribbons, the CIB twice, the Silver Star, and they expected first modesty and then bravery, bravery told modestly, modesty exhibited bravely, and they were rewarded with uncertainty. He could sense, almost feel, their disappointment; he found himself talking about how cold it was and pissing on his carbine, and they wanted to hear about how he had killed with a knife; but he had never killed with a knife, in fact, never killed with the carbine on these missions. His great miracle, his great act as an infiltrator, was staying alive and most of that was beating the cold. The IBM machine must have sensed this because, instead of being assigned to a Special Forces twelve-man unit and the special guerrilla war and infiltration duties, *Green Berets*, he had been converted to an average American Adviser (would they tell that to the ROTC students, he had thought, that he had failed to get a Green Beret and that he was just another adviser, would the light that he had lit flicker ever so slightly?), sent mercifully to the flat country instead of the mountains. The thought of climbing mountains at his age and slipping into Laos (he had never wanted to visit Laos, anyway) terrified him, and if he was thankful for anything in his life, it was that at least he was in the Delta.

He thought of a day this hot in the mountains and the fear came back to him. It made walking in the Delta a little easier.

Anderson came alongside him, and Beaupre questioned him about the Colonel, did he think the Colonel seemed a little nervous today.

Anderson said no, he hadn't talked with the Colonel, but the messages had been the same: were the troops bunched up? Had Beaupre and Anderson said anything about their bunching up? Was the heat affecting the troops? What was the reaction in the villages? Any good signs, any bad signs, any signs at all? Was Dang any better? Any worse? Were the troops alert? What did the crops look like? Did they need anything? The messages were the same as ever; he was on their ass no more, no less, than usual.

Beaupre, looking for signs of hidden conversations with the Colonel, nodded and said the Colonel was too smart a man to push it too much on a hot day.

Then deliberately, as if hiding his need of water

were something to be ashamed of, like an alcoholic proving he was not an alcoholic, Beaupre took
his canteen and took a long drink of water while
the Lieutenant watched.

"This goddamn country," Beaupre said, "has
the worst tasting water in the world. You think it
tastes bad because the geniuses of the United
States Army have placed chemical after chemical
in it. But you're wrong. It tastes just as goddamn
awful without the chemicals. Actually the chemicals sweeten it just a very little bit. The problem,
of course, is ancestor worship. You see, these here
people always bury their ancestors in the best part
of the land which always turns out to be near the
wells so when they are drinking water, they are
really toasting their ancestors. The ancestors just
don't taste so good, that's all. Well, everyone knows
that, I mean, they may be stupid but they're not
that stupid, you see. The real problem is polite-
ness. They're a very polite people, you know that.
Well, it's a well known fact that someone can't
smell himself or taste his own ancestor, so he
doesn't know his ancestors taste so bad. But he
goes to his neighbor's house and the water there is
terrible and the ancestors taste like hell, but he's
too polite to say anything, I mean, you can't go
over to Dang's house there and drink the water
and make snide remarks about his grandfather,
can you?"

He walked a few steps more. "That's the trouble
with this country," he said, "the water and the
people smell the same."

"Don't let the psywar people hear you talking
about the people like that," Anderson said. "They're
real close to the farmers."

He was amused by Beaupre now in conversations like this. He never knew which way it would go, whether Beaupre was serious and bitter, or being funny, or a little of each; in the latter two cases he could relax and enjoy it, but sometimes in the first it turned sour and he had to be careful; he played his role with Beaupre cautiously now.

"Screw the goddamn psywar people. They all work for the goddamn VC, anyhow. Every week they come down and tell us how to be nice to these people, be nice, be friendly, be gentle, don't turn the nice little friendly peasants into bad VCs. Be nice to the peasants and understand them because they had a hard life and their mothers didn't love them enough. Crap like that. You ever see a psywar gentleman on an operation? Shit, it happened one time when I first got here, and we were moving along and ran into a little trouble, wasn't even an ambush, just a few VC popping away with old French rifles and rubber bands. So the Viets started to fire, it was small enough that they weren't frightened and this psywar gunner was firing more than even the goddamn Arvin. He didn't know what the hell he was shooting at. I believe he was holding his weapon up and just pressing away to beat hell. He was scared shitless, but finally either the VC went away, or by mistake we even killed them, you never know, and he was there just thanking the hell out of me and saying what a hell of a guy I was and brave and cool, you know, the usual. But then the sonofabitch went back to Saigon and he wrote this report about how bad the area was, Charleys everywhere, and making it seem that the reason it was so bad was that we had behaved badly right from the start and hadn't treated the peasants nice and right and didn't give them enough psywar. Feed them more psywar, he said. He reported about me, too, and there wasn't anything about me being a hero like I expected. He described me as being unsympathetic to the aspirations of the people and not likely to win either their hearts or minds, and surly. Surly!"

"Bad weekend in Saigon, huh? Too much of it," Anderson said. He was loyal to his wife, and went to Saigon only for PX supplies, or to see a movie, and then only at the express command of the Colonel who was fond of him and worried that he was taking the job too seriously, and thus forced him to leave the Seminary.

"Oh, sure," he said, "rough weekend. But never too much of it." It was one of his official roles at the Seminary, the swordsman (only two kinds, good and better; the only thing I regret about what I did when I was younger was not doing more of it, etc.). The Colonel never encouraged Beaupre to Saigon and indeed delighted in referring from time to time to Beaupre's marriages, his first (or American) wife, his Saigon wife, his Cholon wife, his Saigon Number Two Wife. Which one gets your allotment, Beaupre, he would say. Beaupre had taken to going to Saigon almost every weekend in recent weeks, the Vietnamese usually observing a truce on Sunday. He went to get out of My Tho as much as to get to Saigon ("the only man in My Tho who will risk five ambushes for one hairless Indo-Chinese piece of ass," the Colonel said); the only trouble was that when he arrived in Saigon despite his reputation as a swordsman, he had difficulty in deciding just exactly why he had come after all, why he had spent the time arranging to get free, the risk driving up the highway (as much avoiding the Vietnamese bus drivers as the VC mines); after that, all that happened was that he spent all his money, drank too much watered whiskey and fake French cognac, and wandered around the city sweating heavily alone with thousands of other sweating American wanderers. But he had gone; it had been a three-day weekend, in honor of one of those innumerable Vietnamese holidays ("the day of homage to the dead goat," Raulston had called it); he had driven in with three others, but slipped away from them when they entered the city, staying on the outskirts of Cholon in a cheap hotel far from where the other Americans, and particularly officers, stayed. It was a hotel inhabited by a few Vietnamese civilians, officials from the boondocks apparently, some visiting Chinese merchants from Singapore, and occasional Special Forces people, down from the mountains, arriving in groups of three, staying up all night, fighting, drinking, and screaming— memorably one conversation: "I call police. I call Vietnamese police. You no good. I no fraid you, but I call police." Then a scream, and a shout and a voice: "You call you goddamn hoooore and I'll make them check you out for the fifty-seven goddamn kinds of diseases you're carrying," then more screams and laughter and silence. The Special Forces people had three days and stayed drunk the entire time until on the morning of departure, a truck was sent by to collect them, still drunk, and take them to their own airline at Tan Son Nhut, to be restored, still drunk and unshaven, to their tiny outposts near the Laos border; it was, they claimed, the great glory of Special Forces, they didn't insist you spend the last day on a pass sobering up, all they wanted was the body.

There was no soap in the room, no towels, and the toilet paper was so sleek that the Special Forces people used to steal it in great quantities to take to their camps to shine boots. But at the Hotel, unlike the Continental or Majestic or Caravelle, he could bring a girl to his room, and he didn't have to be with the same officers that he had just roomed with all week at the Seminary (knowing what they looked like naked, and which of them brushed his teeth and which didn't. He knew all this of them, and they knew all this and perhaps more of him and he was not anxious to have them around with him in Saigon, so that everything would be reported back to My Tho). Here there was at least a hint at privacy. He had brought women to his rooms a few times, prostitutes, some of them pretty, but he had been uneasy and then somewhat sheepish about the elaborate precautions he had taken hiding his money and his real identification, as though somehow one racket wasn't enough for them, that some sort of second racket must also be involved. So these occasions with the whores had not been memorable; successful certainly, but symbolic in that he had never returned to the same girl twice. Never during his weekends had there been (not love, of course) even enough passion for a second try; they arrived, they performed, and they disappeared. He could not remember their names, but more, of eight of them he could remember the body of only one and that only because she had a Vietnamese-size body and American-size breasts and had seemed to fall asleep in the middle of the

act. The last weekend in Saigon had been one of
the worst. It had started Friday night; he had
begun by walking into a Cholon restaurant alone,
had looked across the room and had seen Big
William, who shouted: "Well, look what the Good
Lord Jesus Christ and his Vienamese counterpart,
the Lord Buddha, did send Big William for dinner, Big William's friend Captain Bopay, and Big
William knows that Captain is a good cat."

Beaupre, not entirely sure whether he was pleased
to be with Big William, sat down. It was not that
he had strong feelings about the Negro, he liked
him more than he disliked him (though he did
identify him with Vietnam, they were all tarred by
that brush, no one could be loved here), but he
liked privacy on his Saigon weekends. They ate a
good meal, and Beaupre, more than he realized,
bitched about the country and the war, and Big
William tried to cheer him up.

"You got to swing with it, baby. Course it ain't
what you thought it was, or what you wanted.
Course it ain't that. If it was what you wanted,
nice and warm and all that, you wouldn't be here,
man. Big William knows that. But you can't fight
it, that's something I learned a long time ago in
another country, that's the way it is. It was like
that afore you got here, it's like that now, and it's
going to be like that when you and me are gone,
departed and left, and so there is only one rule,
swing with it and smile. Even when Big William
doesn't swing with it, he smiles so these people
here, they think: There's Big William and he's
swingin' with it. And they think, oh, that Big
William, that is a swinger. You do that, and you
keep in mind Big William's other rule, which is,

that if this place were any good, why we wouldn't be here. There be nice things and pretty things here, why there'd be a law against people like you and me comin' here, maybe only politicians and such could come, and the Vienamese got to have these Senators and Congressmen for counterparts. You do that and you be all right."

But Beaupre remained depressed and a little bitter, and Big William seemed concerned for him.

"It ain't that bad, baby, it just ain't that bad. Ain't that good, course, but ain't that bad. Ain't but one worst thing can happen to you here which is that one day you and me we're out on an operation and this Vietcong sees us, but he lets Big William go by because he likes black cats, and feels badly about them havin' to go around poor like they do in Alabama, wearin' nothin' but black pajamas, and he zaps your white ass dead. That's the worst, see, and so they send you back with this flag, and right away you a hero. Man, a big funeral, and a band playing sad songs about you, and a big headline, very first page of the newspaper sayin', Our Captain Bopay is a number one Hero, and tellin' how you was a hero and killed all these Vietcongs until they kill you, and they print this big picture of you, not smiling but lookin' very herolike. And, man, evruhbuddy cry over you, girlfriends you got some off of, and girlfriends never gave you any, all of them cryin'. That's the very worst can happen. All right now, you take *Big William*, and that same Vietcong is waitin', but instead of zapping you, he lets you by because he likes white cats, and he zaps *Big William* because he heard about how all the black cats own *Cadillac*

cars, and he don't like none of that shit. Well, first
thing, the war end right there that minute for Big
William. And then the next thing they send his
black ass in the biggest box they got, and all the
gravedigger boys complaining because his ass is so
big and it causing them trouble because their
boxes ain't *the right size*. Well, they ship this back
the slowest way they can, and year or two from
now, maybe this war *even over,* this box get back to
Pickens, Alabama. Ain't no Pickens band for Big
William, no sir, and the Pickens Citizen States
Press they put the story on page fifty-seven, which
is the page devoted to *What Our Colored Friends Is
Up To,* and there at the bottom is this little story
and ain't no picture, and this story says that Big
William, Black Colored Negro Male, who the Army
say come from this here city is dead, over there in
some Asiatic country, and no mention of being a
hero, and then it goes on to say, how about that,
we always said it would happen that way if this Big
William is the one we're thinkin' of because he was
always causin' trouble, and when he was here he
was mighty uppity, and it wasn't any bargain the
Army got, and let that be a lesson to all of you. So
it ain't so bad for you except that the both of us is
violating Big William's number one first law which
is to swing with it, so we better go to this here
swinging bar Big William know."

They left, Big William talking about the bar,
insisting it was the best in town ("only the king
swingers go there, man"); Beaupre had wondered
whether he belonged there; the Negro saw the
question in his eyes and was puzzled by it at first,
and then shook his head and said not to worry
about *that,* this bar was for swingers, even the

police who waited outside were the best police swingers in town.

On the way to the bar, Big William had confessed that the reason he liked this bar was the Mammasan; she was still the best of the lot, all woman, not one of these little chirping flower girls, but a woman, and for him she was free and, in fact, sometimes he stayed in her apartment which was a hell of an apartment, more air-conditioners than a general's house, with five or six houseboys, but all of them like *midgets,* smallest people you ever saw, even for Vietnamese people, all kinds of good silk things on the bed, and silk clothes for him to wear, and then all these drinks with fresh fruit and brandy in the morning. It swung over there, not a bit like Pickens, Alabama. The Mammasan was a hell of a woman and wanted to marry him, he said, but who the hell wanted to spend the rest of his life in this country, even wearing silk things on a silk bed, and drinking fruit and brandy in the morning. Although, as he said, the Mammasan would put Big William in business too; she would open up a couple bars for him.

"You imagine it. Every time some GI gets himself a piece of ass, white GI or colored, Big William gets a slice of it. Big William become the king of this city. Bars named after him, maybe name one bar after Pickens, Alabama, honor of Big William's birthplace. The Pickens Bar. Big William gettin' richer and richer and helping all these GIs, Big William better than the USO."

Beaupre thought he was lying, but when they got to the bar and walked up the stairs and knocked, the door opened, and the Mammasan came, and saw the Negro and said: "My beeg

Weellyam" and kissed the Negro, and then very politely shook hands with Beaupre.

"You have been faithful to me, my William?" she said.

"Ah Mammasan, Big William is as pure as when he left you," the Negro answered, and added, "though it ain't necessarily his fault."

Beaupre was led into the bar by the Mammasan and was stunned: there was no one there but Negroes. The entire bar was Negro, tall ones and fat ones, Negroes who were obviously officers, and Negroes who were enlisted men. He had never seen anything like it before; it was like being in another world. The girls were all Vietnamese, running around in their antiseptic white costumes, looking somehow like they were nurses for these men. Was it his imagination or did the Vietnamese girls seem lighter; were they lighter because the customers at the bar were so much darker, or were they lighter because the Mammasan who was obviously very clever went out and hired girls especially for their light skins.

Beaupre shivered and seemed to stop. Big William seemed to move a little closer to him. Nevertheless Beaupre quickly felt the tension and the stares.

There were two waves of silence: first a wave as the Negroes stopped talking, and then a second, somewhat delayed wave as the Vietnamese girls realized that something was happening and that they were not supposed to talk. Finally one of the Negroes, a tall thin one, elegant with a face like a black American Indian (Beaupre was sure that he was an officer, and found out later that he was an enlisted man, a specialist of some sort), turned, half to them and half to the rest of the bar, so that he was facing neither, and said:

"Captain Redfern, why don't you just introduce us to your Division Adviser there? Tell us that colonel's name."

"Eben," said another, "that ain't any colonel. That's a general. That's General Harkins. Big William brought us General Harkins."

"Ain't General Harkins, either," said the first, "General Harkins a slim young fella."

In the background Beaupre could hear one Negro say to another, just loud enough so he could hear, "What do you think it is?"

"A VC?"

"Don't look like any VC I ever saw."

"No, but remember VC goin' to look different in the bar. No black pajamas when they're on pass, remember."

"You think so."

There was a moment of pause and then another Negro, wearing an expensive sports coat which tapered out at the shoulders and in at the waist, said, "Gentlemen, you think this general meets the entrance requirements for our club? Captain Redfern, you have not, I hope, forgotten that we are strict here, yes sir baby, very strict."

Everyone was laughing except for Beaupre and the Negro. Big William turned from Beaupre and walked to the bar.

"This man Big William's friend. This man come here with Big William. This man ask Big William, 'Big William, is it okay if I go with you to this number one best bar you been talkin' about?" And Big William say, you are my friend, and it is all right because the cats there, they swing just like I told you, they swing plenty, but in addition, *they is all gentleman cats.* And then Big William add, this here is one place in this here fucked up country *ain't fucked up yet. Ain't been ruined yet.* And now lookahere what you done. You made a liar out of Big William, and so right here now, at eight forty-seven o'clock pyem, Big William apologize to his friend Captain Bopay. I apologize."

Then someone shouted and told Big William to stop talking like a white Baptist preacher, and someone else brought Beaupre a drink, saying "Here you are, General," and he was for a moment accepted.

After a while the Mammasan came in and took Big William by the arm and pulled him away. The Negro turned to Beaupre, saluted and said: "She got some brand new silky things ready for Big William and so I got to surrender. Bye bye and be brave, baby. I'm off to my silky death."

At first Beaupre felt as if he had been left in a dentist's anteroom, and was just about as calm. But the Negroes were very pleasant, bringing over a girl and introducing her to Beaupre. One of the Negroes said something to her in Vietnamese, and she giggled.

"He's calling you a white Senegalese," another translated, and added, "They call us all Senegalese. At first they thought all colored people are Senegalese, and it wasn't any big compliment because it seems the Senegalese kicked the shit out of them when they were here back in the French war, but it's something of a joke now."

Beaupre bought her three drinks and smiled at her and held her hand, but he was still unsettled by the entire experience and he wanted to leave.

He would have sworn they were all speaking a foreign language and that this was a foreign country (Vietnam, after all, was not a foreign country, it was Vietnam, it was theirs); the atmosphere was hazy and strange as if time had stopped; it was as if the Vietnamese girls were like Americans, like him and the Negroes were the foreigners; in the background a Vietnamese band was playing rock and roll on its electric instruments, but the sound too was foreign, it was playing such a driving Negro blues and rock that the music was alien too, as though it was more African than American; it was as if the Negroes had brought the band with them from Africa.

She said her name was Thinh.

"Tan?" he said.

"No," she said, "Thinh."

"Oh," he said, "Thin."

"No," she said, "Thinh."

"Thin?" he said.

"Yes," she said.

Most of their conversation was similar; he didn't particularly want to make a date with her, he could do a lot of things, but he couldn't do *that*. But they had been very nice to him here, and he was embarrassed and afraid to leave without somehow trying to set something up, fearing that the Negroes would take it as racial, which it was, and become annoyed. So at great length and rather publicly, he began to make a date; at first she didn't understand him, so one of the Negroes who spoke Vietnamese came over to help him out; they were being so helpful that he felt even more embarrassed, putting so much energy into a rendezvous he had no intention of keeping for the next day in front of the Majestic. The date being set, he continued to drink, the Negroes surprisingly friendly to him by now, and when he finally left, the thin one, the interpreter, took him back to his hotel, and, sensing his feelings, said, "Look man, don't feel bad, it ain't *that* bad, we like it this way, we have our choice we do it the same way; you take the Mammasan, she don't bullshit us, and we don't have to drink that water-whiskey. Mammasan, she give us the real cognac brandy, same for the girls. You go down the Catinat with the white cats, nothin' personal and I ain't against it, but they pay *500* Peas for one piece. Five hundred Peas and them so small. Shit, here we pay 150, 200 Peas, same thing, just as good, some of them better; 500 Peas, we don't pay our Vietnamese cook up at Dak Pek that, and he's got just as good tits as most of them."

Beaupre nodded, oh it was fine, fine he said, he liked it a lot, he'd come back.

"You do that, because the cats, they like you, they like you fine, they be hurt you don't come back."

Beaupre was appalled by the evening, yet finally touched by it too: appalled that that world existed and that he had entered it and touched by their attempts to retrieve it, and wondering for the first time how they felt every time they went into his world. And he wondered what happened to the silk pajamas when Big William was in the field.

The next day he had skipped the appointment, sure that if the girl had kept the appointment at all, which he doubted (he never believed these people ever kept their word on anything, never were on time for anything) someone would pick her up. He wondered if it would be a white officer (only officers stayed in the Majestic area) and what he would feel if someone told him she had come from Big William's bar. He had wandered aimlessly around Saigon the next day, eating Chinese food at two restaurants, visiting several bars, watching with some sadness how grown men, officers, men with wives, were handled so coolly by the little seventeen-year-old bar girls, who would play two boyfriends off against each other, the tension at the bars rising, the officers vying to buy the whores more drinks, the cheap tea-tasting whiskey-colored substance that they poured away and were repaid for. He ended up the evening at a place called "The Beautiful Tea House." The bar was a giant horseshoe and there was only one seat open. He was sitting by himself, without a girl; next to him there was a bald American speaking Vietnamese, a psywar type, Beaupre decided; the psywar people spoke the language, had lots of money, and got the best girls. He was talking with a pretty but tough-looking Vietnamese girl. She began to stare at him, and after a minute began to speak to him in Vietnamese. The bald man, not an American at all, but an Australian, apologized for interrupting Beaupre's peace and started to interpret for him:

"She says she thinks you're very handsome. She says she's nineteen years old which is a bloody lie, and from the north which is probably another lie, and that she'd like you to buy her a drink, which is the bloody truth, mate."

He bought her a drink, and the Australian continued to translate, taking an evil delight in this ("she says someone as brave as you must have killed many, many Vietcongs. Of course, Yank, we don't know what she tells the bloody VCs about you"); then finally the Australian turned with some resignation toward Beaupre, saying: "Look, mate, I spend the whole bloody day changing these languages until English sounds as crazy as Vietnamese, and I have more trouble with my own language than theirs. But the thing is, I'm free now, and if you and the lady don't mind, I'm going to work in only one," and he went back to talking with the girl in Vietnamese. In a few minutes another girl was summoned; faceless at first, except for glasses which made her unique among the bar girls, like their schoolteacher. "Says she speaks some English," said the Australian, "don't believe it very much."

In a fashion she spoke English. Beaupre was intrigued by the glasses and the prim look it gave her; it gave him his first sexual excitement of the long day. They all wore white dresses, that was the prescribed legal uniform, but they wore them so short and tight, that it was almost obscene (so tight that their panty lines could always be seen, and the helicopter pilots, who were insane for military abbreviations, had invented the phrase VPL, for Visible Panty Line). Later he remembered vague outlines of the conversation: he, trimming his age by five years, severing himself from any previous marriage, making himself, he decided afterward, remarkably innocent; he, asking questions about her family—she lived at home with her parents and four sisters. A good deal of the time must have been spent talking about her housing problems, because moments later when the girl disappeared, summoned momentarily to entertain a new arrival (Beaupre, suddenly jealous, felt himself like the other officers he had mocked earlier in the day), the Australian turned and said:

"Not my place to butt in, mate, but don't take them straight home at night. Doesn't work. Not the right form. Country's got too many rules, and it's more efficient in applying them against the crumpet than the Communists. Very easy for the white mice to pick them up in this city at night, particularly with you Yanks, and the mice can be pretty tough on them, you know, police station or gang-bang, take your pick, lass. Mind you, they'll do it for you, go home with you, they're like that, very agreeable little crumpet. It's not fair though. Afternoon's the best. They're free then, and they're just another upper class girl out for a stroll with a Yank, except maybe better dressed. No one bothers them."

Beaupre and the Australian talked on, with the Australian becoming increasingly friendly; he was at ease with the Australian the way he would never be with another American. Out of it had come this suggestion: the Australian would be away at Cap St. Jacques the next day and Beaupre was welcome to use his apartment to meet the girl. He had accepted and had mentioned it to the girl, Lim Fung, and she had been obviously pleased. The Australian had been very precise in giving them both instructions and handing Beaupre the key.

Sunday he had been as nervous as a young boy, sure that she was not going to come, sure that she was going to come and be pounced on by the police the moment she entered the apartment. She was fifteen minutes late, and when he was

sure that she had played with him and had no
intention of coming, she showed up, wearing tight
stretch pants, a tight blouse, and no glasses.

He remained nervous: the uncertainty of being
in someone else's apartment, the thought of the
police outside, the cold sharp temperature of the
room because of the giant air-conditioner (later he
would remember the temperature and the noise
of the air-conditioner first and the girl second), all
combined against him. In the daylight her English
seemed less adequate; that which with the smoke
and the whiskey had passed for communication
seemed more perishable now. They tried to speak
for several minutes: each time he said something,
he sensed that she heard it completely wrong (I
am glad you are here; you what? I glad, happy
you here. You not happy I here? No, I happy, very
happy you here. I sorry). So they went to the bed.

"Banan," she said, giggling, and at first he thought
she was mocking him, and then realized that she
was simply talking and being friendly.

"Banan, yes," he said. He performed badly.

"You no like Lim Fung," she said.

No, he said, he liked her fine, but again the
more words he said the more confused she became. He tried again, but in the cold he could not
work, and he could not even sweat. He tried to
sleep, hoping to wake up stronger, but in the
sunlight and with the air-conditioner, he could
not sleep and seemed all the more restless for his
attempt. He was unsuccessful for the rest of the
afternoon, increasingly restless, not even sweating.
She no longer talked of the banan, or pointed to
it. It was, he thought, not even guilt which had
stopped him. At the beginning, she had pointed

first at him, then at herself and jabbered: "Like you, like me, like you yes." Now she had stopped it.

Now she began to talk about Kim Chi: "You like Kim Chi, Kim Chi like you. No like Lim Fung, no like you," until he decided that Kim Chi must be the other girl, the Australian's hard-looking little friend, and that she thought he preferred Kim Chi to her; so he began a long protest, pointing out that he didn't like Kim Chi, that she wasn't his type. At the beginning he spoke only in their mono-talk, but as he became carried away by the idea, he used more and more words, and more and more passion, until she was completely confused by what he was saying. In turn she started walking around the room and picking up the magazines. Most of them were old copies of *Playboy*. She was delighted with them and with the center spread. She stood naked in the little room, holding open one of the center spreads with its American-style and American-size voluptuousness. She was smaller, equally fine, rather like a miniature model of the pose; the girls who eat whole wheat bread and the girls who eat rice, he thought. She asked him something: he thought she asked if she looked like one of the models, and he nodded and said yes. She appeared delighted and walked around the room posing, holding the giant naked blonde beside her. She mimicked the exact pose, and he laughed and clapped his hands and in response she did a little dance. For a moment there was some life in the room. Finally she asked if she could keep the nude; at first he said no, but then her face fell; and so he said yes; after all, he had disappointed her enough that day. She tore the centerfold out, dressed quickly and left the apartment happily. He waited for her to leave, and then he slowly dressed. He was sure the Australian would notice the missing pinup and would think that Beaupre had stolen it (did one, after all, leave a note saying sorry about the missing photo, but the Vietnamese whore liked it so much), and had thus repaid the kindness. And so he left the apartment and his newly found bar, two more places that he would never return to.

"I figured you were a little more tired than usual," Anderson was saying. "Must have been a rough weekend. So much of it in Saigon, you had to fight it off, huh?"

"Yeah," said Beaupre, "that's the tiring part, fighting it off."

"I hear you had to fight one of them wore glasses and looked like a schoolteacher."

"Where'd you hear that?" said Beaupre grinning, the grin acknowledgment of his success.

"Oh, you know. There aren't any secrets in this country. All your other girlfriends know about it too. How was it, pretty good?"

"Well, you know how it is about women with glasses."

"That true, huh?"

"Even here. Worse here." Grinning, "Or better here."

"Goddamn, I always wondered about that. You have to pay here."

"Supposed to, but first she said she didn't want any money. You know, the next time though they ask you to go to the PX and buy them hair spray, and the next time after that you have to get them hair spray and stockings, and then the next time it's hair spray and stockings and nail polish and perfume and a goddamn sweater, and cigarettes for their father, and canned milk for their sisters' babies. So I give her the damn piastres. Simpler that way. That way they don't own you."

"Sounds like they want to marry you," Anderson said.

"No, not marry, they don't expect that, except with some of these young troopers. No, they just want to own you, and make sure their little friends working next to you at the bar don't get to own you. They love each other a lot. Just like American girls."

They walked together in silence for a few minutes, Beaupre ahead of Anderson. "God, I bet you haven't walked this much since World War II," Anderson said.

"Not as much then. We didn't know how simple it was, and how good we had it. Sure we walked, but in a straight line. Boom, Normandy beaches, and then you set off for Paris and Berlin. Just like that. No retracing, no goddamn circles, just straight ahead. All you needed was a compass and good sense. But here you walk in a goddamn circle, and then you go home, and then you go out the next day and wade through a circle, and then you go home and the next day you go out and reverse the circle you did the day before, erasing it. Every day the circles get bigger and emptier. Walk them one day, erase them the next. In France you always knew where you were, how far you had walked, and how far you had to go. But this goddamn place, Christ, if I knew how far I had walked, it would break my heart. From Normandy to Berlin and back, probably."

Then he paused, walked on, and said, as though to himself, remembering this for the first time, thinking of it with fondness (it had never struck him that way at the time), "And France, France smelled so good."

Chapter Four

AT ELEVEN-THIRTY they were moving haphazardly along the canal, one of those peaceful moments when earlier fears were forgotten, and when it was almost as if they were in some sort of trance from the heat and the monotony, when they were fired on. Three quick shots came from the left, from the other side of the canal. They appeared to hit short, and they landed near the center of the column, close to where Lieutenant Anderson was. He wheeled toward the bullets, spoke quickly in Vietnamese, taking three men with him and sending a fourth back to tell Thuong what he was doing—not to send anyone unless it was clearly a real fight, and he could hear automatic weapon fire; they were taking no automatic weapons, Anderson said.

He sensed that it was not an ambush; you trip an ambush with a full volley of automatic weapons fire—to get the maximum surprise firepower and effect, you don't trip it with a few shots from an M-1 rifle; the fact that the sniper had fired so quickly, Anderson thought, meant that there was probably one man alone who wanted to seem like more than one man. But damn it, he thought, you never really know here, you tried to think like them and you were bound to get in trouble: you thought of the unique and they did the obvious; you thought of the obvious and they did the unique. He brought his squad to the canal bank, and two more bullets snapped near them. *Ping, snap. Ping, snap.*

He told one of the Viets to go above him on the canal bank, and one to stay below him, and one to stay behind him as he waded the canal. They were to cover him as he crossed, and they were not to cross themselves until he was on the other side; he didn't want all four of them bogged down in mid-canal when they found out there was an automatic weapon on the other side. They nodded to him. Do you understand me, he asked in Vietnamese. He turned to one of them and asked him to repeat the instructions. Surprisingly the Vietnamese repeated the instructions accurately.

"The Lieutenant swims?" the Viet added.

"The Lieutenant thinks he swims," Anderson said, and added, "do you swim?"

The man answered: "We will all find out."

Anderson waited for a third burst of fire, and when it came, closer this time, he moved quickly to the canal bank and into the water, sinking more than waist high immediately. As he moved he kept looking for the sniper's hiding place; so far he could not tell where the bullets were coming from. He sensed the general direction of the sniper, but he couldn't judge exactly where the sniper was. He was all alone in the water, moving slowly, his legs struggling with the weight of the water and the suck of the filth below him. He knew he was a good target, and he was frightened; he moved slowly, as in a slow-motion dream; he remembered one of the things they had said of the VC in their last briefings ("The VC infantryman is tenacious and will die in position and believes fanatically in the ideology because he has been brainwashed all his life since infancy, but he is a bad shot, yes gentlemen, he is not a good shot, and the snipers are generally weak, because you see, men, they need glasses. The enemy doesn't get to have glasses. The Communists can't afford 'em, and our medical people have checked them out and have come up with studies which show that because of their diet, because their diet doesn't have as much meat and protein, their eyes are weak, and they don't get glasses, so they are below us as snipers. Brave, gentlemen, but nearsighted, remember that.") He remembered it and hoped it was true.

Ahead of him all he could see was brush and trees. Remember, he thought, he may be up in the trees: it was another one of the briefings: "Vietcong often take up positions in the tops of trees, just like the Japanese did, and you must smell them out. Remember what I'm telling you, it may save you your life. You will be walking along in the jungle, hot and dirty. And you hear a sniper, and because your big fat feet are on the ground, you think that sniper's feet are on the ground too. But you're wrong, he's sitting up there in the third story, measuring the size of your head, counting your squad, and ready to ruin your headgear. They like the jungle, and what's in the jungle? Trees. Lots of 'em. Remember it, gentlemen, smell them in the trees."

Anderson had left the briefing thinking all Vietcong were in the trees; even now as he walked, he kept his eye on the trees more than on the ground.

Behind him he heard the Viets firing now, but there was still no fire from the sniper. He reached the middle of the canal where the water was deepest; only part of his neck, his head, and his arms and weapon were above water now. He struggled forward until he reached the far side of the canal. He signaled to the Viets to hold fire, and then, holding his weapon in one hand (he did not want to lay it on the canal bank, suppose someone reached out from behind a bush and grabbed it), he rolled himself up on the canal edge, but there was still no fire. He punched through the first curtain of brush, frightened because he did not know what would be there (Raulston had once done this, pushed through and found to his surprise a Vietcong a few feet away; they had looked at each other in total surprise, and the Vietcong had suddenly turned and fled—though Beaupre in retelling the story claimed that it was Raulston who had fled, that the Vietcong had lost face by letting him escape, had lied to his superiors, and that Raulston was now listed on Vietcong rolls as having been killed in action, and that Raulston was now safe because they didn't dare kill him again).

He moved past the canal and into the dense brush, found what looked like a good position, and fired off a clip to the left, right in front of him, most of the clip to his right, and finally, for the benefit of his instructors, for Fort Benning, the last one into a tree nest. Nothing happened and he reloaded and moved forward. Then there were two little pings, still in front of him, though sounding, perhaps it was his imagination, further away. But the enemy was there, and so, encouraged, he began to move forward again, his senses telling him that the sniper was slightly to his right. He was alone, he had kept the others back at the canal bank; they would be no help here, for they would surely follow right behind him and he would be in more trouble for the noise they would make and for being accidentally shot from behind, that great danger of single-file patrolling; yet going like this, he sensed terribly how alone he was—he was in *their* jungle, they could see him, know of him, they could see things he couldn't see, there might be more of them. He moved forward a few yards, going slowly both by choice and necessity in the heavy brush. If there had been a clock on the ground, where he left the canal and entered the jungle, it would have been six o'clock, and he was now moving slowly toward one o'clock. He kept moving, firing steadily now. From time to time he reversed his field of fire. Suddenly there was a ping, landing near him, the sound closer, but coming from the left, from about eleven o'clock. The shot sounded closer, and more excited and frightened now, he moved quickly in that direction, feeling the brush scratch his arms and his face (he couldn't use his hands to protect his face, they were on his weapon); now he squeezed off another clip, two quick ones, three quick ones, the last three spaced out, a musical scale really.

There was no answer and he pressed forward, the jungle still around both of them. Then he was answered again, the mating call, two little pings, the VC's weapon had a lower pitch than his, and the sound—and this made him angry—was coming from the right, near one o'clock, where he had just been. He cursed under his breath, and moved quickly to his right, realizing even as he pushed ahead that he was doing a foolish thing, that he was violating all the rules he had been taught, that he was offering an American officer to a trap, that he might be taken prisoner; at Benning they had warned against that, don't be captured, there was too much psychological advantage the VC could take, showing him around in the villages.

Still he pressed on, angry, frustrated. He thought the VC was mocking him, playing a game with him; you didn't do that in war, war was not a game, you didn't screw around, play jokes with rifles. He fired off another clip toward one o'clock and moved there. He continued to plunge forward. But there was nothing there. Then there was a ping from the left, back at ten o'clock. He moved a little to his left, but he didn't fire. A few minutes passed while the Vietcong finally grasped his message, that Anderson for the time being was not going to fire. Finally there was a ping, from eight o'clock this time; the sniper was behind him. But he couldn't fire in that direction or he might hit one of his own men. He waited and waited and then charged toward six o'clock, ready to fire at point-blank range. But nothing happened.

Suddenly there was a ping ping from eleven o'clock. He turned and fired angrily, shouting: "Come out, you sonofabitch, come on, come on out. Fight. Come on, I'm waiting, I'm here."

He waited but nothing happened. Did he hear a giggle? He made the same challenge in Vietnamese, but it sounded foolish to him. No giggle this time. There were no more shots. He checked his watch. He had been gone ten minutes. He waited two minutes more, and nothing happened. Still angry, he went back to the canal bank, and collected the other Viets.

"Sometimes," said one of them, "Vietcong are like the pederasts. Don't feel so badly. It is their game."

Anderson nodded grimly, and they crossed the canal in single file; Anderson much taller than the Viets, his head barely above water, was amazed; just as much of them showed above water as of him.

"The war is good for the leeches in the canal," said one of the Viets, "that is all. A full meal for them today."

He nodded, and then moved back to the main path. At least they would be able to move quickly, while catching up with the rest of the unit.

Anderson came upon them quicker than he expected. They had stopped and were gathered around a very small Vietnamese. They had formed a circle and the Vietnamese was standing with his hands up and his back to a tree; Dang was standing in front of him, towering over him, and Beaupre was behind Dang, towering over him. They get smaller and smaller, Anderson thought. As he approached, he heard Dang saying, "Murderer, we have caught the murderer. VC dog. The dog."

"Got to be one of theirs," Beaupre said. "Doesn't

weigh more than fifty pounds. All ours weigh more than that."

Dang was in charge of the interrogation. "A Communist VC," he said to Anderson, "part of the ambush plot against us."

"He means the little scouting party you just went on," Beaupre whispered.

"Proceed with the interrogation of the Communist Vietcong prisoner," Dang told Thuong. "I will assist when necessary."

The suspect said he was Hung Van Trung.

"Of course that's his name," Beaupre told Anderson, "they all have that name, that or Trung Van Hung or Hung Van Hung." His age was fifty-eight.

"The Communist is probably lying about his age," Dang said, "these people lie about everything."

Suspect said he owned a water buffalo: "Rich bastard, eh," Beaupre said when Anderson translated, "usually they don't even own a goddamn chicken by the time we catch them."

He came from the village of Ap Xuan Thong.

"Is he a Communist? Ask him if he is a Communist." Dang shouted and the prisoner began to mumble, a rambling guttural chant which seemed half song and half prayer.

"Tell him we are interested in his relationship with Ho Chi Minh and not his relationship with Buddha," Dang said.

A corporal slapped the prisoner. He was loyal to the government, he insisted, he was sometimes a government agent.

"Knees are too bony for one of ours," Beaupre told Anderson. In fact the prisoner said he was in trouble because the local Communist cadre which was headed by Thuan Han Thuan ("How can the VC chief have the same name as our man there?" Beaupre said), suspected that he worked for the government and had taken his wife away last night when the Communists had come; when he mentioned the cadre chief's name, he paused as if expecting that this would confirm his story.

Dang asked him for his identification card, and he could produce none, and Dang slapped him. He claimed the Communists had taken it and he was slapped again. They asked him about children. He said he had three sons, and mentioned daughters, but seemed unsure of the number. Of the sons, he said, one had died of a disease. Which disease, he was asked; the yellow disease, he answered, and they all nodded *yes, the yellow disease, that one*, though later it turned out they were unsure exactly what the yellow disease was.

"Yellow disease," Beaupre said when told, "everybody in this goddamn country's got that. How the hell can you die from it?"

Two of the other sons had served with the government forces; he believed one was dead and one was alive.

"What units?" Thuong asked, the tone of his voice reflecting his boredom with the interrogation. The prisoner said he did not know the units, but they fought against the Vietminh, he was sure of that.

"Tell him that it is not the Vietminh, it is the Vietcong," Dang said, and the corporal slapped him again.

"Now tell us what happened," Thuong said, "and try to make it as honest as you can. Show us your heart is pure."

The prisoner nodded and began: he had worked long that day and had gone to bed early. It was the rainy season and there was more to be done this year because of last year's drought.

"Ask him what he had for breakfast," Beaupre told Anderson, "go ahead. Speed up the interrogation."

The prisoner was interrupted by Thuong who told him to hurry up with the story if he wanted to live to finish it. He had gone to bed early when he was called by Thuan Van Thuan.

"Is he a neighbor?" asked Thuong.

"No, he lives three houses away," said the prisoner.

"Sweet Jesus," said Beaupre. "The prisoner said he knew it was trouble right away."

"Why," demanded Dang, "because he knew all his Communist friends were coming? All the dogs were coming?"

"No," said the prisoner, "because Thuan's voice was loud and commanding"; he stopped, and it appeared for a second that he was going to say, commanding, like the Captain's, but then he continued. Usually Thuan's voice was soft and supplicating, an attitude he did not trust because Thuan was not honest. He claimed to have an electric box, the only one in the village from which he received special messages from Saigon and Paris and Hanoi; the prisoner was sure it was a false electric box. Thuan had been arrogant and had demanded they come to a meeting; Thuan had insisted that his wife come too, which upset him since she had been sick and coughing and had finally fallen asleep, but Thuan had given them no choice and so they were taken to the center of the hamlet, where lamps had been lit, and where there were twelve visitors, all men. He knew right away they were soldiers.

"Did they have any weapons?" Thuong asked.

"I didn't see any," he said, "but I knew they were there."

"How does he know?" Dang asked. "Because he is one of them."

"Because of the way the men behaved," he said, "men who have guns behave one way and men who do not behave another."

He seemed puzzled that they did not understand the distinction, and asked Thuong: "You have never talked with a man with a gun when you don't have one?"

"Good question," Beaupre said, "the son of a bitch is telling the truth."

The suspect stopped as if waiting for someone to slap him; he said the men had talked about politics and said that the long noses (he looked embarrassed at Anderson and Beaupre) were coming to the village the next day and would try to kill all the people. Then they had served tea. He himself had taken two glasses. He had wanted to take only one, but had been afraid if he took one, this might offend the Vietminh.

"Vietcong," Dang corrected, less angrily this time.

Some of the others had taken three cups.

"See how many cups he'll take from us," Beaupre said when Anderson translated this.

The next day he had been told to go north from the village, because the Americans were coming from the south, east and west, and for that reason he had slipped away and gone south. Thuong asked him about his wife; she had been kept by the Communists as a bearer and as a hostage. Thuong continued to ask questions about the enemy, and Beaupre pulled Anderson aside and told him to get on the American radio and quickly call the information in; he did not trust the Viets; if it were left to them, the intelligence might not reach the CP until the next day.

"He was telling the truth, wasn't he?" Anderson said.

Beaupre didn't say anything for a minute. "Yes," he finally answered, "he's telling the truth. That's the worst thing about it. Makes you long for the usual ones, who've never seen a VC, never heard of the war."

He walked on a few yards. "A rock and a hard place. That's where we are, between a rock and a hard place."

He felt dry and thirsty and a little nervous; he had mocked this operation from the start, and most of his fear had disappeared with the selection of Big William for the helicopters. Now he was becoming frightened again, aware of his age and the senselessness of the war—not the killing but the endless walking each day and the returning to My Tho with nothing done, nothing seen, nothing accomplished, nothing changed, just hiking each day with death, taking chances for so very little, wondering if he were going to be sold out, wondering whom you could trust. He had not distrusted people in World War II. He had been assigned to an infantry regiment and he had fought with a variety of men, some had been good soldiers, some weak, some brave, and some cowardly, some who had loved the war, and most who had hated it, but whatever, there had never been a quality of distrust. It had been simpler there, even in Germany, where you hated everyone, but once you entered the villages, you were not loved and kissed, you were not ambushed or tricked or betrayed. The distrust had begun in Korea when suddenly it was more than a matter of fighting and killing, instead it was a matter of wondering where you were going, and whose intelligence had set it up and who was paying, was it only one side: a matter of looking into the face of the man when you finally met him, and perhaps looking for too much, seeing things which didn't exist, and looking for things which had no right to exist, which probably had never existed. "Don't expect our Korean agents to have blue eyes and blond hair and friendly smiles," they had told him, "they don't. They don't look like Marines. They look like gooks because they are gooks. Don't you worry about who they are or the way they look. You let us do the worrying. All you have to do is keep the goddamn loose change out of your pockets because it makes too much noise on cold winter nights out there, that and trust your compass and your own good common sense. We don't expect you to like the Koreans, that's not your job." But compared to this country, Korea was simple: here you began with distrust, you assumed it about everything, even things you thought you knew. Even the Americans seemed different to him now, and he trusted them less; in order to survive in this new world and this new Army, they had changed. Yes was no longer exactly yes, no was no longer exactly no, maybe was more certainly maybe.

"I think we may be getting ourselves sold out," he said, and then added to Anderson, one of the few kind things he said that day or any other, "you be a little careful now. Hear?"

There was a terrible quality of truth to what Thuong had just heard and he did not like it; he had not liked the operation from the start and he had always disagreed with Headquarters and Staff over the area. Staff called it a blue area (the Americans, he decided, loved maps even more than the French and had taught them about red, white and blue areas; the Americans loved to change the colors, to turn red into white and white into blue, to put red pins on white spots and blue pins on red spots) and blue was supposed to be secure, but Thuong had never liked the area; he did not operate there often and so he tended to accept the Headquarters' version of the area as being secure, only to find once they were in the area that it was not quite what it seemed, that it was always a little more hostile than the authorities claimed. He suspected that it was a Communist area where the guerrillas did little in the way of challenging the government and were content to rest somewhat tranquil on the surface, using it as a communications path. The Arvin recruited, Thuong remembered, few government soldiers from the area, and the young men they did take showed a higher desertion rate than might have been expected.

He walked beside the suspect, near the rear of the column. "I believe you have told us the truth," he told the prisoner.

The man did not look up at him.

"Perhaps you will be free by the end of the day," Thuong said.

"Perhaps we will all be dead by the end of the day," the prisoner said a little bitterly.

"Would you like some of my water?" Thuong asked.

The prisoner said no, but then asked if Thuong would do him a favor: "You believe me and know what I say is true." Thuong said yes, he would do the favor, if he could, depending on what it was.

"Would you tie my hands together?" the prisoner asked. "You see if they see me walking with you . . ."

"I know," Thuong said, and ordered his hands bound; the Americans, he thought, should have asked this peasant whether he thought the area was blue or red. Perhaps they should explain that it was safe to walk free, that it was blue.

"You are not from here, are you?" the prisoner asked.

"No," said the Lieutenant, "I come from the north."

"I know, but you are not like the other northerners, you are nicer than them."

"Only because you are more honest than the other southerners," he said.

Thuong trusted the man although he did not trust southerners in general; he thought of them as dishonest, a little too lazy for their own good, a little too willing to tell you what you wanted to hear, always dependent on their women to do their work (almost, he thought, a pride in this, the best man was the one whose woman worked the hardest). He thought of northerners as being more honest, although the northerners who had come south like himself were no longer particularly honest; they had to bend enough themselves in order to survive.

Thuong was thirty-one, though, like most Vietnamese, he looked younger to foreign eyes. He was slim and his face seemed almost innocent; he had been in the Government Army too long to be innocent, eight years, and all of them either as aspirant or lieutenant. His lack of advancement was no particular reflection on his ability, indeed, those few superiors who took the time to monitor his file, such as it was with more papers missing than enclosed, were surprised at the degree of achievement and ability; having achieved this surprise, however, they did not feel obligated to increase his rank or command. Indeed the older he got, and the more papers there were in praise of him—including, dangerously American praise—the more it tended to mitigate against him; here after all was a man of ability who had not gotten ahead. Therefore, there must be something wrong, something unseen but known, something political; his superiors were in particular surprised by his father's choice of religion. His father, having associated with foreigners in the north, did not choose to convert; he worked closely with foreigners and dutifully accepted their pay and their orders, but not their religion. This was unusual for the time; there were, after all, many Vietnamese who began to dress like the French, eat like the French, and talk like the French. His father referred to them all as the "mustache-Vietnamese" in honor of their copying French-style mustaches. Thuong had once gently asked his father about this, why he had never taken their faith, and his father had said simply that he was paid for his manual contributions, not his spiritual ones. Nevertheless, he was closely associated with foreigners and during the beginning of the French war, he had continued to work for them, as much by accident as by decision (he did not particularly like them, but he had a vague feeling that since everyone else was deserting the foreigners, it was improper for him to do it as well); one of his objections after all to the French had been the contempt they had showed toward Vietnamese people and their obvious belief that all Vietnamese were cowards, to leave now would be to confirm all the worst things the French had said. When the foreigners by their stupidity, which his father could not have been expected to have foreseen, lost the war, thereby proving to the French that all Vietnamese were not cowards and making his father's original reason somewhat obsolete, it was decided to split up the family and come to the south, splitting up into small groups so that they wouldn't be stopped by the local Vietminh bands.

The way had been difficult from the start and Thuong's grandmother, who was in his charge, had nearly died from exhaustion. (Later Thuong remembered trying to find water for her, giving her all his water, and the terrible thirst that had stayed with him for days at a time. When he thought of the division of the country, he thought of his own thirst.) When they finally arrived in the south, they turned out to be among the few Buddhists who had made the trip, and were immediately placed in a camp for Catholic refugees. There they shared the difficult position of the Catholics of being unwanted immigrants in the south, without sharing either their faith or their protection.

On the basis of his father's connections, he had managed to attend a military school, after first lingering on the waiting list for a year and a half. There he quickly discovered that he was a northerner in the south, a Buddhist among Catholics, and thus at almost any given time lacked the proper credentials. The southerners did not trust him because he was a northerner, the Catholics did not trust him because he was a Buddhist. In a country shorn of idealism and reeking of cynicism and opportunism, he was an object of suspicion. So he remained a lieutenant; as they remained suspicious of him, so he in turn became distrustful and cynical about them. He accepted the legacy of being his father's son with the same fatalism, largely because he could think of no real alternative to it and because if it offered nothing else, it offered him a certain sense of privacy and individualism. He went along with their rules but he tried to remain himself. He envied the Communists their self-belief, their ideology, their certainty, even their cruelty; the Catholics, their convictions and connections; the Americans, their intensity and idealism; and his father, his gentleness and enduring innocence. (His father, embarrassed and uneasy and unworldly, periodically would ask him if he *had* to be a soldier, wasn't there something else he could do; his father knew, of course, that it paid well...); he doubted what he did and he suspected that the war would probably be lost. It was not that he wished to be on the other side— that would be easy to do, a short walk away during an operation—nor that he thought the other side more just: the Communists, after all, had killed an uncle, just as the French had stupidly managed to kill a cousin, wiping out a village (until then pro-French) as the Vietminh had planned for them to do. The Vietminh side was as cruel as the French, and lacked only the corruption of the French. He suspected that ten years of power would improve their sense of corruption (depending, he thought, on the degree of success of their system; they would need a certain amount of success to be corrupt. If their system failed, they could retain their integrity). The danger of going over, he thought, would not be that he had been fighting them all these years and had killed many of their people (they, unlike the Arvin, would have real records and they would know who he was, and who he had killed); nor that after the minimal comfort of My Tho, with its soda pop and iced beer, that life would be too rigorous. It was simply that he knew he was too cynical for the passion and commitment their life took. To gain religion in Vietnam, he thought, you must start very young; to retain it, he thought, you have to be very lucky.

So he did his best at being a lieutenant. He told Anderson, the young American, that he was twenty-five instead of thirty-one in order to avoid embarrassing the young American; Anderson had been surprised, he had thought Thuong much younger. Thuong took a certain limited pride in what he did; more, almost in what he did not do, in that he did not play the game of promotion and did not attach himself like a barnacle to his superior officers, did not call in prolonged artillery barrages on villages before the assault. But the dominant feature of his life remained his fatalism. As his father had somehow made these fatal flaws, deciding at one strange moment to keep a false sense of integrity (false, thought Thuong, because both he and his father had made so many other demeaning decisions and accepted so much other fraud during their life-times), Thuong had continued relentlessly and recklessly down the same deserted path: there had been, after all, chances to convert. Others did; it had been suggested to him. There were many new Catholics in his class at the Academy, and now several were captains, and one was a major; but there was for him in conversion a sense of surrender, he had admired the Catholics when they were the minority in the north, but now that they had come to the south they had changed. What had struck him as quiet courage, now often seemed to him to be arrogance, and the converts were inevitably the worst.

So he continued his own way: he did not desert because it would hurt his parents (and also because it would make no difference to him) and so his life had made him a very old lieutenant. The particular reward that he now enjoyed for his fatalism was Captain Dang. The Captain was a year younger than Thuong and had been in the army for a shorter time, and was soon to be a major, according to Dang himself. He was well connected in Saigon and was aware of this; he visited Saigon frequently, and he often referred to the dinners and parties he had just attended. He frequently praised Thuong (in front of Thuong, implying that he had also praised Thuong in those same great halls); he talked of promotion for Thuong, something, Thuong was virtually sure, if it ever came, would come in spite of Dang. Dang did not know the name of anyone in the unit below the rank of corporal; he cheated on the ranks, regularly turning in more men than he actually had, failing to report losses (the advantage being that he was not reprimanded for losing men, and at the same time continued to draw their pay. The result was that the company which should have been understrength by ten men was usually understrength about two dozen, and the pressure on the men was even greater than it should have been). Thuong had compensated for this in part by commandeering an extra light machine gun from a friend in another company: the company had lost it, then captured it back in a long battle with the Vietcong battalion. Since it had already been reported lost, it was surplus on the rolls and Thuong had been owed a major favor by his friend—he had lent them three men during a key inspection. Thuong was careful to pay as little attention as possible to Dang's corruption; Dang, indeed, was convenient for Thuong. He fitted Thuong's own view of what an officer was, what the system was, and made his own lack of promotion easier to bear; it would have been more bitter were Dang a real soldier. But for two years and a half now, he had despised Dang over one incident. It was a time just before the American helicopters had arrived with their remarkable ability to bring in reinforcement, and there was still a terrible isolation to battle: you were hit and you stayed there alone and fought it out. There had been an ambush, a brief and bitter one, and Thuong at first had been paralyzed like everyone else, sure that he was going to die there; but he had in those first minutes seen something he would never forgive and never forget (particularly since when he saw it, he expected it to be one of the last things he ever saw): Dang taking off his officer's pips. If you are going to wear the pips in the great halls of Saigon, he thought, you must wear them in the U Minh forest.

Chapter Five

IT WAS NOT just the heat, Beaupre thought, struggling badly now, it was the heat and the boredom. The boredom was part of it too. He was numbed by the heat, occasionally dizzy now, losing his war to it, alone in this struggle. He had seen the others: Anderson, watched him drink, seen the tilt of the canteen, almost full. The Vietnamese lieutenant, Thuong, didn't even drink, Beaupre was not even sure he carried a canteen, perhaps he did. Beaupre never saw him use it; Dang with very small stains and often none at all, a good choice for a counterpart, perhaps that was why they had picked him. Beaupre tried to drive the thoughts of the heat out of his head, but they always returned. That was the other terrible part of the war, the boredom, no one to talk to, eight hours in the field if they were lucky, fourteen when they were not, and no one to talk to all that time. Oh, he thought, a few words to Dang, perhaps one hundred: Yes, Captain Dang, no Captain Dang, fine Captain Dang, please Captain Dang, very good Captain, Americans think, Vietnamese want, You, Us, You, thank you Captain.

Perhaps two hundred words. Anderson, okay to
talk to Anderson, but not eight hours' worth,
lucky if thirty minutes' worth, against division
rules for much longer, the Colonel didn't like it,
you people don't go out on these operations to
interview each other and find out where your
wives came from, you're not here to talk to Americans, you're here to talk to Vietnamese. The
Colonel was absolutely right, he thought, the Colonel, he was sure, spoke to Co for a total of ten
minutes a day. Yes Colonel Co, no Colonel Co,
You, Us, Vietnamese people think, American people feel, Saigon, Washington, good, bad. He felt
dizzy.

They came suddenly to a clearing, and the
Vietnamese, unannounced, no orders heard or
given, only obeyed, suddenly decided to take a
break (Beaupre heard no command and could
never tell about these breaks, didn't know if the
Vietnamese officers ordered these breaks, and the
men followed up, or the men simply took the
breaks and the officers thereupon followed up
and gave the orders). Normally he hated these
endless breaks; he could never adjust his rhythm
to theirs. Whenever he wanted to move, they
stopped; whenever he wanted to stop, they moved,
scurried, laughed, double-timed, ran. But this time
he was grateful: he was numb with the heat, dizzy
now and desperately afraid of being sick. His
uniform was soaked, and his face was covered
with sweat, a mask, red on the surface, covered
with a thin layer of his sweat, with dust and filth
mixed in with it, and his beard alive and vibrant
in the dense lush tropics of his face, growing like a
jungle plant. He moved for the coolest place, near

the water, he thought, and near a tree. He pulled out his canteen; there was very little water left, and it was now very warm from the overheated canteen. He licked his own sweat when he was through.

Anderson came up to him and sat down and asked for a cigarette.

"You don't smoke. What's the matter. This place drive you to that?"

"No," Anderson said, "leeches. I've been through too many canals today and now that big canal back there, and I think they're having dinner. On me."

"One Beaupre cigarette survival kit coming up," Beaupre said and opened his shirt pocket. He brought out a strange-looking package, a small metal container packed in a good old-fashioned American prophylactic; Beaupre kept his cigarettes in the container to prevent them from being crushed, and a rubber band around the container to keep them from getting wet. He didn't mind, he said, his sandwiches getting wet in the paddies, indeed it improved the taste, it was like ketchup, but he couldn't stand or smoke wet cigarettes. The others had mocked him at first, but now a few of them had adopted the trick which they said prevented the cigarettes both from getting wet and from carrying diseases.

Anderson lit one and then started unblousing his pants: he had tried desperately to keep the leeches out. Elastics. Double elastics. Stockings up to his knees. Stockings and inner stockings. Nothing had worked, always the leeches had won; they were brilliant, they circumvented everything, they came, they nestled, they fed. Once he had found one near his crotch and had almost fainted. Now he looked at his legs, the soft underside, the white meat which they liked so much; and at first he failed to see them. Then he saw them, one on each leg, huge, bloated with his own blood.

Beaupre saw them too. "Well, you were right about them eating dinner. You got a feel for them now. That's some consolation," he said.

"Look at them," Anderson said, "ugliest things in the world."

"Well, they're good ones. I don't think I've seen bigger since I've been in the country."

"I hate them," said Anderson.

"But you got to look at it from their point of view," Beaupre said. "Just like in psywar. You've got to understand them. Now they think they're medics. They've read all their own publicity and their history books, got themselves sure as hell brainwashed, and they see themselves not as blood suckers, not that at all, but as life savers. They're here to save lives. They're improving relations with you. Giving you first aid, and they put on their very best for you, biggest ones they got. Biggest I ever saw, even in a country like this which is known for its small people and big leeches. You're a lucky boy for just a lieutenant."

"I hate these goddamn things," said Anderson, pulling feverishly on the cigarette and applying it to one leech like a tiny blowtorch.

"Shouldn't talk like that. Look at it a different way. Think of it as an honor. Now you take Big William. He has this leech problem. They won't bite him. Never. Won't touch him at all, and him a captain and bigger than you, with probably a lot more blood. He told me there wasn't a single leech on him ever, and he was thinking of taking it up with the civic action people and maybe higher. He said it smacked of racism, and here you are, only a lieutenant and complaining."

He watched Anderson push the cigarette into the leech. "Well, if you must, boy. Okay give it to him. Now, boy, now. Push. Go right in there! Don't be afraid. Don't let him stare you down. Don't let him look love at you now. Don't back down now. Harder, harder, that's it, there he goes. Give it to him now, now you've got him. He's retreating! Oh, you whipped his ass, you did. Well done."

Anderson, his face white because he truly hated leeches, the sight of them feeding off him, eating him and drinking his blood, repelled him terribly. He had become accustomed to most of the agony of this country, the dead men, faces ripped open like melons, the sick children whose heads and faces were covered with scales (though he wept the first time he saw that), the women so thin that they seemed to be dying in front of him; he had become accustomed to all that, yet he still hated the idea of the leeches, and if he could have brought himself to it, he would make someone else get rid of them so he wouldn't have to look. But it was not something you could admit.

"Well, I must admit that was well done," Beaupre said, "I mean he was in there. He was so sure he was helping you, he really dug in. Dug in so much he's going to leave a scar. He really did some surgery on you."

"They don't bother you?" Anderson asked.

"They're afraid of me. I poison them. A few of them have tried, but I got them all. They're allergic to me. Maybe they're trying to tell me something. Here you are, old buddy, take yourself another cigarette for the second. Leeches that big, you deserve a cigarette for each one."

Anderson lit it and went to work, but the leech refused to budge. Anderson tried; he made the cigarette tip red coal hot, but the leech held on.

"I don't mean to tell you your business," Beaupre said, "but you're going after the wrong end. You're burning his tail. You got to get his head. He'll never move that way."

Anderson looked at Beaupre, sure he was putting him on. 'How can you tell which end is which? You don't even know if they have two ends. Don't give me that." He went back to burning the same end.

"Of course they got two ends. They're like everybody else," Beaupre said. "If you can't tell which end is which, why you just try the other end. Then see what happens. You don't have to, of course, don't have to listen to me. It's not my blood."

Anderson tried the same end once more. The leech remained. The next time he tried the other end. The leech began to move. Very slowly. Anderson gave him the cigarette again. He moved quicker now.

"Well, here you are. You got the right end this time, just like I told you."

Anderson looked at him, perplexed, wondering if there really were two ends to a leech.

"He was a mean one, though," Beaupre was saying, "that one had more blood than a first aid station."

Then almost as if he were talking to himself, Beaupre said, "Jesus, I feel terrible." He shut his eyes, and he felt terribly dizzy for a moment.

"Don't crap out on me here in Ap Than Thoi," Anderson said.

"That where we are?" Beaupre said. "I might have known. Got a little dizzy." He opened his eyes.

"Well, it doesn't look as populated as Ap Than Thoi," Anderson said, "but we checked on it, and it is. Smells about the same."

"Well, that's the important thing. That's how you can tell. They can always change the other thing, disguise themselves, put up a sign on the city limits with a different name, take down the police station, put up more flowers, but they can't change the smell."

Ap Than Thoi was the missing village: they had missed it six weeks ago on an operation and since then it had become a legendary place. It had been a search and clear operation and they had been warned that the local population might be un-friendly, which, in the particular understatement of the times, meant that they were likely to be very hostile. They made their first stop as scheduled with a minimal amount of success and difficulty, and then they had moved toward their next objec-tive which was Ap Than Thoi, four kilometers away, and reputed to be most unfriendly. They had gone the four kilometers, and they had not found it, and they had gone a little further, an-other click and a half and they had not found it, and by then the Colonel was on their radio de-manding to know if they were in Ap Than Thoi, and if not, why the hell not. A few minutes later he was back on the radio wondering aloud why they were behind schedule, saying that it was goddamned embarrassing at Headquarters, embarrassing to the entire American Army, but more important, embarrassing to him, in front of his Asian allies. Beaupre, he said, his voice becoming very correct, was making him look silly in front of Colonel Co, and the Colonel *did not like to look foolish in front of anyone, particularly his Asian counterpart.* It's embarrassing here too, Beaupre had said, and Dang is just as embarrassed as I am. Don't tell me about Dang, the Colonel said, I don't want to hear about your problems, get those ffing Viets off their asses, that's your job. You're not paid to be embarrassed. You're paid to move.

Ten minutes later when they still hadn't reported in from Ap Than Thoi (by this time Beaupre had convinced Dang to send patrols out in all four directions, looking for Ap Than Thoi, and Dang had complied surprisingly easily, apparently Co was chewing his ass too over the failure to find the village which was making Co lose face at the CP), the Colonel came back on shouting angrily that if they didn't get there, he would come in to Ap Than Thoi himself, by helicopter, he would by God welcome them there and be the goddamn hospitality committee; he would lead their goddamn parade for them and he would carry out on that same ffing helicopter Beaupre's weather-eaten ass, and that shiny new West Point ass too, Anderson's ass, he said a moment later, having forgotten the Lieutenant's name in his excitement. That was when Beaupre had gotten angry. "My weather-eaten ass is now resting at," and then read his coordinates, and demanded the coordinates for Ap Than Thoi. The Colonel read them back and they were the same. Beaupre then was angry and excused himself to the Colonel, begging his pardon sir, and announced that they were there, but the village was not. It was the village's fault. He also referred to it as "your Ap Than Thoi."

He sensed from the voice that the Colonel had taken it relatively well; he had read coordinates out, where they were, where they had been, where they were going, and finally again demanded to know where the village was.

"Beg your pardon, sir," Beaupre said, "but there are two Americans and one hundred and fifty Vietnamese wondering the same thing."

"The other side of the canal," the Colonel said, "that's it, the other side of the canal. The map made a mistake."

"Beg your pardon, sir," Beaupre said, "but the map did make a mistake, but it's not the other side of the canal. We've been working it for the last twenty minutes and they don't have it either."

"But there must be a village there, must be people there. Why we even have reports saying the people are hostile, so that proves it. If they're hostile, they've got to be there," the Colonel insisted. "Look around yourself, Captain Beaupre, what do you see?"

"Sir, Vietnamese, a lot of them, a lot of trees, some bushes."

"What are the troops doing, Beaupre?"

"Sir, the troops are sitting down, and talking and some of them are already impurifying the canal, and a few of them are starting to break out the rice."

"Just a minute," the Colonel said. "You wait there a minute, Beaupre, and don't go anywhere.

Don't leave the place you're at. Think of it as Ap Than Thoi."

Then he sent a spotter plane over and it circled the area for a few minutes without finding the village or drawing fire. Finally the plane radioed back and the Colonel called Beaupre and said, "Beaupre, cross Ap Than Thoi off your map. Forget about it. It's not your fault, Captain."

Beaupre thanked him (he liked the Colonel) and made a note that someone should draw up some new maps, since these were twenty years old and not always accurate.

That night the Colonel said nothing, but apparently the entire advisory group knew what had happened and almost overnight Ap Than Thoi became a part of the vocabulary. One went away to Saigon but claimed he was going to Ap Than Thoi; someone violently ill for three days claimed he had contracted the bug at Ap Than Thoi; if an officer with a girl met a buddy in Saigon, he always introduced her as being from Ap Than Thoi; if something went wrong in the field, a terrible snafu, it always took place at Ap Than Thoi; if an operation were being planned and someone wanted to know the local political climate, he would be told it was no worse than Ap Than Thoi.

"Old Ap Than Thoi," said Anderson. "I wrote my wife the other day and said I had a big leave in Ap Than Thoi, and I spent one hundred dollars because the hotels are so expensive there, fifteen dollars a night and ten bucks for meals, and then I said there was a lot of incidentals because it cost so much there, but that I couldn't list them and so she wrote me back this long letter saying it was all right and she understood about the incidentals; she knew what it must be like to be a soldier and she only hoped I had a good time there, and then she asked some of the other wives where Ap Than Thoi was because she never heard about it, and one of them said it was a Chinese whorehouse—she said house in her letter—in Saigon, and another of them said it was a little island where the French soldiers used to go for girls; and so I wrote her back to tell her what Ap Than Thoi really was and thinking it was pretty funny and I got back the angriest letter I've ever had, telling me not to play games and she was heartbroken, and how could I do this to her, and now all the other wives were laughing at her, and how did I really spend the one hundred dollars."

He looked over at Beaupre and kept talking: "Can you imagine that, her getting pissed off at me for not getting laid, so I knew I couldn't joke about it or play any more games any more so I gave Crawford a check for one hundred dollars when he went to Hong Kong and told him to buy exactly one hundred dollars' worth of this new stereo gear, and he did and I wrote her a letter saying it was all supposed to be a surprise but I spent the hundred dollars on stereo and tape recorders, and I got back a letter saying wasn't I wonderful and she had loved me all the time."

He looked over at Beaupre. "Goddamn women. If I told her there never was any hundred dollars, she'd never believe me." He looked again. "You know, Captain, it's not my job to say this, but you sure look like hell today. You been in this business a lot longer than me, but you ought to go easier on it in Saigon. You're pushing it awful hard, considering the kind of climate and all that sun."

He waited for Beaupre to curse him, and then he thought, that old son of a bitch is asleep, too much whiskey, more even than I thought, and then he looked again and saw something different: Beaupre's mouth a little bit open, a faraway look in his eyes. He's passed out, Anderson realized.

For a moment he thought of calling the CP, and then he realized that would be the worst thing he could do; for a moment at least it was none of the CP's business. He looked over and was disgusted by this old man, his face dirty and unshaven; whoring, and drinking and belching on weekends, he thought, then coming down to his job and going on a little walk, and drinking too much water and passing out like some Navy officer. It was a hell of an example to show to the Vietnamese; the Vietnamese did not drink heavily, and he believed they were repelled by Americans drinking: what can they think when we show them men like this—we come here to set examples for them, examples of the greatest army in the world, new, modern, with helicopters, and we bring them Beaupre who shouts and curses and who can't walk as far as their own women and who comes apart in public. He was offended by that part, in particular, the public failure of Beaupre; failure was permissible but not desirable as long as it was private; when you came to the time to fail, you stayed out of other people's sight. You didn't do it in a foreign country. Let him do his failing at the bar in the Seminary. He was sure the Vietnamese could smell the whiskey in Beaupre's sweat just as he could. A few minutes ago Beaupre's face had been red and now it seemed a dirty white. He felt the canteen and it was virtually empty; Beaupre had drunk all his water before noon, like a kid cheating on candy. Anderson took his own canteen which was virtually full and poured half the water into Beaupre's canteen. Then he cupped his hand, poured a little water into it, and sprinkled it on Beaupre's face. He watched the water trickle down, making tiny rivers of cleanliness on the face as it washed away some of the filth. He did it again, and then once more, and then he noticed a little movement in Beaupre's eyes.

"You're okay," he said. "You're okay, old buddy. Don't worry, all okay now." His hand moved slowly again to Beaupre's face and his voice was surprisingly gentle; curiously he was no longer disgusted by the old officer, but in a strange way that he did not entirely understand he felt for him; the hell with the Vietnamese, if they saw it and didn't like it. Beaupre might be an old fool, but he was our old fool, he was an American fool, an officer too, and he had seen many wars and many places and if this war were a little better organized and better run, if they would shape this goddamn war up a little, he probably wouldn't drink so much here either. It was their fault as much as ours. Beaupre had earned the right to drink that much.

"You're okay now. Just a little hot here. You know how this place is. God giving the Vietnamese all his leftover sunshine. Heat getting all of us. Getting me too. Getting the Viets. You've got to get up so you can help carry the Viets out of here."

Beaupre seemed to nod.

"Heat's terrible," Anderson said. "Worst day I've seen here. Another damn hot day but we're going to lick it."

Beaupre, he thought, seemed to be coming to, seemed to be nodding. Anderson held the canteen out for Beaupre, but carefully so that the Captain wouldn't drink too much, and then quickly pulled it back. He waited a minute and then gave Beaupre the canteen again.

"I hate the heat and I hate the sun here," Anderson said. "Funny thing, I grew up in Minnesota, and it was cold there, always cold, and I loved the sun. We used to wait for it. I remember even in the late spring it was a big thing when the sun finally began to come because it meant that when you got into your car after school, the inside of the car would be warm, and then you would wait until the middle of summer and finally the sun would come on strong, and I would go swimming and lie down and wait and enjoy the sun— not go into the water at first, but instead let the sun broil and broil me until I was soaked in my own sweat, completely covered by it, and only then, I would go into the water. It was like a game with the sun. I loved it so much. After this country, I'll never be able to do it again, never be able to let the sun hit me again, without thinking of Vietnam and wondering if I'll make it through the day. I'll never do it again."

"I passed out," Beaupre said.

Anderson patted him on the shoulder.

"That's a hell of a thing to do. Never did it before. Never crapped out before."

"Happens to everyone on a day like this. You'll probably have to carry me in later."

"I'm sorry, shouldn't have done it to you. Never did anything like that before." He paused. "Dang see me?"

"No," Anderson said, sure that somehow Dang had managed to see Beaupre, that this was the kind of thing Dang would know. "He's too busy talking to the generals."

"Look," said Beaupre, "I'd appreciate it if you don't say anything about it back at the CP. It's the first time. You know how those people are. That's the kind of thing they love."

"They're all too busy sleeping back there anyway. They never tell us when they tap out."

"That goddamn Dang. I bet he knows."

Anderson brought out some salt tablets and told Beaupre to take two.

"I hate those goddamn things. I won't take them."

"You don't take them and I'll get stuck with Dang for the rest of the day."

"I'll take the one."

Anderson gave him one and then a little bit of water. Then he made Beaupre put his head between his legs.

"Feel any better?"

"Better. The Disneyland movies are over. I'm back in Vietnam, if that's better."

"You sure you don't want me to call a chopper? We could probably get one in here. It might be the best idea."

"I don't want any goddamn choppers. I'll walk in. I've always walked in. The day I don't walk in, they can get the wood box and the American flag ready for me and call the man about the farm. There's only four, five clicks left and I'll make it.

You call a chopper and I'll never go out again. They'd like that, one more retread captain, that's all they need now. They'll put me in psywar and let me inspect strategic hamlets. Eighteen years, and I've always walked and I'll do it today. I took your salt tablet, didn't I? You think I'd have taken one of those things if I wasn't going to walk in?"

"All right, but I just wanted to be sure."

"Well, you're sure now."

Beaupre stood up, a little unsteady at first, and began to walk around. "All right," he said, "now let's get those goddamn Viets off their asses."

Beaupre got up slowly and pulled the visor of his hat down as far as it would go. Anderson offered him a pair of sun glasses; Beaupre didn't like them, they were, he thought, the mark of a playboy, but he took them and put them on, perhaps they would help a little; whatever else, he couldn't afford to pass out again, to be sick once more. If he was, then Anderson would be forced to report him, he knew that. He stopped for a minute by the canal and dipped his wrists into the canal water; it was warm but to him it seemed somewhat cooler than the air and this was an old trick he had learned long ago as a construction worker in times when water was cheap and plentiful, it was like playing with the pulse. Then not refreshed, but not sick, he began to walk again. At first he was careful; each step was like a marker, the very accomplishment of it was an achievement and bore proof of survival; each step meant that he hadn't fallen down or passed out again. Then he realized he was going to be able to walk, that he was going to make it, and he cursed himself for having passed out in front of the boy, for having made a fool of himself, for having had to ask the boy not to report him. He cursed his weakness, but he was sure he was going to make it that day. He realized that Anderson was only a few yards behind him; Anderson was worried and lacked confidence in him. I'll show these young bastards, he thought, and he began to gain back his confidence, and he returned to the normal monotony of the long hot day.

That monotony did not last long. Ten minutes later they were interrupted by the radio. The voice was shrill and excited, so excited, that Beaupre moved right back to the radio without Anderson's having to signal him.

"Big William. Big William and the Rangers just got hit," the radio said. "Big William bought the farm. Just awful there. Oh, God, they got Big William and I was talking to him when he died, just like I am with you. It was awful. He just kept saying, 'they got Big William and his Rangers just like ten pins, just like ten pins,' and then he died. I never heard that before. Terrible. Everything going to hell there. Two thirds of the lead company dead in their tracks. Not a shot fired, and the Viets going crazy and weeping now. Crawford told me it was the goddamnedest thing he ever saw, looked like twenty little Vietnamese carrying off Big William's body and crying to beat hell. Says he never saw them weep before, and some of them saying, 'how they hanging Big William, they hanging fine,' just like he used to. Christ, all hell's breaking loose there."

Beaupre took the radio from Anderson and

started to calm down the CP, give it to me slow, start from the beginning, no, slower. I'm not interested in who's crying, I'm interested in who's alive and who's dead. Please, make it simple, please, and finally put the story together: they had just come out of a village where they had been particularly well treated ("look how Big William's charm work here, they goin' to name this here village after him, name it Big William Village"), and they were in a particularly good mood. Big William claimed they were going to name not just the village but the whole county after him and the CP had said that they couldn't do that because they didn't have counties, so he said fine, make it a province, it sounds bigger than a county, anyway, more like a whole country, and we'll name the province capital Pickens—he was laughing to himself at that—when the VC opened up and caught them flush in the open, and Big William said, 'I'm hit, hit, hit bad, not even one shot, didn't fire one shot, hit just like ten pins,' and then he died. They got some Vietnamese officer too. Short and sweet, the CP said, now (he was recovering) barely time to get the fighter planes in, the VC were gone before they arrived. There was a hell of a time getting the helicopters to go in there for wounded because the first ship that was supposed to go, the pilot was very short, on his last week, and he didn't like the sound of it, so they bitched a little and changed the order and made his ship the second one, and they came in without fire, but there was a hell of a mess and too many Viets claiming they were wounded and trying to get on the ship. Hell of a mess there.

It was settling down now. It was so short that it

was almost over, the CP said. There were no new instructions. Beaupre was to continue as usual; they might want him to slow down, but they would know later. The Colonel said for him not to change his position in the column, said it was bad luck.

"Any pursuit?" Beaupre asked the CP.

"Not really. Trouble enough getting the choppers to go in, and for a while nobody knew who the hell was in command there. All messed up pretty bad."

"Why no pursuit?" Beaupre asked.

"I don't know," the CP answered, "but I figure if they pursued, they're afraid the VC would zap their ass only more so." Then the CP went out, and they were back with their own problems.

"No more silk pajamas for Big William," Beaupre said.

"What's that, silk pajamas?"

"Silk pajamas. It was just something he liked."

"Did you like him?"

"He was better than most," said Beaupre, leaving Anderson to wonder whether he meant better than most Negroes or better than most officers. Big William, he thought, I spoiled even that one. He had been on his way out of the mess hall this morning when Big William came toward him; it was a moment he had been trying to avoid since he returned to the Seminary from his long weekend. Big William was mumbling some kind of song, singing to himself and to anyone within ten feet of him: "bum bum bum de dum bum. Oh, she's so small. Dum dum dum. But she's so *small.*" Black music, Beaupre had thought.

"Oh Lord, what a weekend. I mean Big William,

he draggin' it today. Now that Mammasan, she is historic. That is a historic woman. Make a *monument* to that woman. Never been so tired. Under the monument just put these words. The Champion. That's all. *The Champion.* Finally I have to say to her, 'Mammasan, you a Vietcong. You a damn VC, you tryin' to kill Big William.' Oh Lord, she start tellin' me about some Frenchman he do it umpity-umpteen times, you know the French record, he held it. So I had to stay there until she forget about that Frenchman, and all of that France. Oh, that is some Mammasan." He smiled at Beaupre. "Hey, Bopay, you all right? All the cats, they like you fine. They say for me to bring you back there. How you like it, huh, just like I told you. Big William don't shit his buddies. Big William take care of 'em."

"Oh, yeah, it was just like you said, man, just fine."

"I mean you liked it, right?"

"Oh sure, best ever in Saigon."

But his voice was wrong and there was a new and different smile on Big William's face.

"Hey, what's the matter with you, Bopay." He looked again, for a long time. "Oh, you didn't now, did you. Oh Lord, ain't that one on Big William. Oh, don't that teach Big William not to screw with it. Oh Lord, I thought you was different. Oh, I do apologize. I do. You one, too. Ain't that somethin'. Oh, you mother." And he had walked off, grinning bigger than ever, singing again, "bum bum, oh, she's so small, oh, poor Big William."

Now, he thought, Big William was dead. Beaupre wondered how much of his last day on earth Big

William had spent laughing at him. You spend most of your life letting people down, he thought bitterly.

Beaupre's uniform was wet, not from the rain this time, but from his sweat; the newest salt line on his fatigues went very deep under his arm, a white chalky mark which went deeper and deeper the longer he stayed in the country. In years to come if he wanted to show he had been in Vietnam, he would be able to hold up his fatigue jacket instead of medals. He felt his thirst again, but strangely, this time not so strong, as if for the moment his preoccupation with the war was quenching it. He was sure now they were in serious trouble, and what was coming awake in him was a deep sense of survival. For the moment at least he did not need the canteen; it was as if there were a great reservoir or survival instinct in him which was now being tapped. The troops, he noticed, did not seem to reflect any new tension: at the first village they had tensed up for a moment and acted like soldiers; they had stopped their bab-bling, even the radio man had stopped. When Beaupre had first arrived in the country and heard all the babbling, he had complained about it, and someone, he had forgotten now, but some-one who was getting short, it was the kind of fact that came with getting short, had explained patiently to Beaupre that it was a tonal language and there-fore a difficult language for radio communication, because the tone could easily be twisted and give a different meaning, and it was necessary to repeat and repeat and repeat. Fine, Beaupre had said, he was more ambitious and more determined then, and now tell them to make less goddamn noise, tell them to stop all that goddamn babbling. He was sure that the enemy traced and monitored and fixed all these babbles; the enemy after all could understand the babbles, had learned them at their mother's knees; at the Seminary when he bitched about this, they assured him the enemy did not have the capacity to monitor radios, but he did not trust the enemy and he did not trust the people at the Seminary.

He wished the troops would go faster, would move it out, and he wished he were a real officer, someone who could give commands and then see them obeyed, who could send a patrol here and another there, could make the troops go fast, go slow, be brave, be strong; wished to be hated, to be feared, even to be loved, but to be an officer and in charge. He wanted to go faster, but he could not push them; he tried and he only succeeded in crowding the man in front of him so finally he moved toward the point. If he could not push them, perhaps he could pull them. He liked the point anyway and he did not think it was the kind of place which should be left to the Vietnamese. When he finally got there, he found a squat young Vietnamese; the Viet relinquished his position with obvious pleasure, smiling broadly and thanking the American. Beaupre was able to move the pace up, but he had to keep looking back to make sure he had not lost the rest of the column.

After the ambush Thuong waited for Anderson to seek him out. It was inevitable. It was a ritual.

If there had been a chance, if there were a patrol working the other side of the canal, he would have crossed over and taken charge of it in order to be away. He knew the outlines of the conversation, what he had come privately to call the funeral service: Anderson would express his condolences for the dead men, whereupon Thuong would express *his* condolences for the dead men; then Anderson would talk about the *Vietnamese* dead, a word or two about the Vietnamese officer (did he know him? he would praise him, did he not know him? he would regret not knowing him better), and then onto the sadness of war; Thoung knew it well. When Anderson praised the Vietnamese officers, Thuong had to respond, often in praise of men he despised. He had heard it, of course, from the other Americans before Anderson (though certainly not from Rainwater who believed fervently in the law of averages and gave signs, all too obvious, that if there were an ambush, he was glad it was someone else who was hit), but Anderson did it the best; he was the most sincere, which to Thuong meant he was the worst. Thuong, after all, did not want ceremonies like this held for him in other units. *What was the name of the Vietnamese officer they got? Thuong. Thuong? Thuong. Which one was he, the one with the mustache? No, not that one. I think he was the little one. Which little one? That proud little one. Oh, that one, that Thuong. Arrogant bastard, but a good officer. Yeah.*

Anderson arrived during a break, which one Thuong no longer knew. He could measure them only by the pain in the foot which was worse when they were resting; the foot was hurting worse than ever now, and he wanted to get on, so of course they were taking a break. He wanted desperately to take off his boot and see how white and ugly and perhaps green the foot was, but didn't dare to, not wanting Dang to come by and see the foot and make a fuss, not wanting the Americans to see it either. He was wondering about the color of his foot when Anderson arrived.

The conversation was typical. They took a bad one. They are all bad ones. There is so much killing of your people. The Vietnamese people are accustomed to it now, it is like the sun and the rain; perhaps they would miss it if it stopped. Then Anderson continued; he was so polite and kind and gentle. When Thuong had first seen him, he had thought: ah, at last this is The American, so big and strong and clean, the hair on his arms so blond. Thuong had thought at once how much milk this young giant must drink (one of his first questions, the third time they met, was to ask Anderson, almost shyly, if in America it was true they were able to drink as much as they wanted. They had talked for an hour about American breakfast foods and milk, and it had been one of their best conversations). Now Anderson was talking on about the ambush and the dead, not differentiating between the Vietnamese and the American dead, and this angered Thuong who considered it a deception, how could he really care about the Vietnamese dead. Anderson was sorry about the death of Captain Ho Van Vien; the Captain, it turned out, fell into the category of Vietnamese officers that Anderson had known only slightly and wanted to know better. Ah, if you had known Captain Ho Van Vien better, you would have found out what I know and his troops knew and your big Negro friend knew, that Captain Vien was a *merde*. The French word is very good. He did not bother to learn about his men or this war, and he did not care for the soldiers. If the Vietcong have finally killed him, perhaps it was by accident. I am sorry, he said, to speak to an American about a fellow Vietnamese in this manner, a dead Vietnamese. You will pardon me. He watched the quiet surprise in Anderson's face, aware that their problems and tensions were his fault.

Anderson, who was tougher with Thuong now than he had been a month ago, looked at him for a long moment, and said, "Whatever you say, Lieutenant Thuong." The Vietnamese, Anderson thought, was a strange one: when he had first come to Vietnam and had been assigned to Thuong, he had been warned: Thuong is a good officer, maybe the best young one, but difficult, doesn't like long noses. Anderson had been delighted, it was exactly what he would have asked for, a good officer who was difficult. When he first met Thuong, he was even more pleased: Thuong was obviously intelligent, and soon after that, just as obviously brave. He was sure that this was what he had come to Vietnam for, and he visualized the friendship, visits back and forth to each other's homes. Thuong would come to Benning and stay with the Andersons, perhaps children named for each other.

They had known each other ten days when Anderson decided to invite Thuong to dinner; but even here he was careful not to rush it, and he waited for a month to pass before he made the invitation, deciding not to corner Thuong and push him too fast. He had made the invitation lightly and informally; there was room for Thuong to reject it, but the invitation had been accepted quickly, without hesitation, though with a certain amount of formality, yet even the formality had only served to please

Anderson. It made Thuong seem more Asian.
The dinner had been a curious one: Anderson
decided not to eat at the Seminary, afraid both of
the food, which he sensed' was too heavy and
greasy for a Vietnamese, and afraid also that
someone might say something improper about
Asians (Beaupre might talk about gooks at dinner).
So they had gone to the local Vietnamese-Chinese
restaurant where the Americans went, nicknamed
"The Purple Plague" in honor of either its lavato-
ry walls or the post-dinner problems. No one was
quite sure. When they finally arrived there
Anderson had a moment of doubt that he had
chosen correctly, and that perhaps this was a
restaurant shunned by Vietnamese, which it was;
but Thuong skillfully guided him in (having eat-
en there before with Americans and being very
dubious about the political loyalty of the owner,
who was excessively friendly with Americans and
spoke English very well). Anderson had gone
there with the specific idea of getting Thuong to
talk about the country and the war and his own
life. Thuong, relentlessly polite and courteous,
but he did not talk about his own life or his
country. Finally it was Anderson who did all the
talking. It was not quite a monologue; Thuong
kept punctuating the conversation with just enough
questions to keep it going: about America, about
West Point, even Germany. Tell me, do the German soldiers really wear the helmets that we see
always in the movies? The questions were very
polite, but sometimes Anderson had the feeling
that he was talking with a much older person,
someone's grandfather who had no interest at all
in the subject at hand, but who was well-trained

in the art of being polite. Thuong left Anderson completely bewildered, not knowing whether Thuong had been completely bored or whether he was anxious to soak up every bit of knowledge possible (Anderson periodically asked a question, such as: do you think the helicopters are helping the war, and he would be answered, ah, but Lieutenant Anderson, you know better than I. The helicopters are from your country). Thuong, of course, was a polite man and so he reciprocated the dinner. He waited several days and then asked Anderson to dinner. Anderson was pleased and proud, perhaps, he thought, the first evening had gone better than he thought. Perhaps it only took time to know someone like Thuong. They were shy, that was it. It took time to show Thuong that you were different, you were sincere, that he was not a gook.

The dinner had been preceded by chance by one of the unit's rare major battles, an attack in which they had first faltered and then performed disgracefully. It had been a day and a night and a day again of terrible and hysterical bitterness and fear and death—of fear being passed among them in the confusion like a great contagious disease, of men groaning and dying and screaming in both languages, of Americans shouting to get those sons of bitches moving, the Vietnamese saying again and again it was not the right time, they must pick the right moment, the Americans saying, no goddamn it now, or we'll all die in this stinking wet hellhole, and the Vietnamese saying not now, we must wait, take cover, and the Americans shouting, there is no goddamn cover, and always the wailing and the shivering in the background. Forty-eight hours later with the anger and the bitterness of the battle still very much alive (even the Colonel, that model of good relations, had told Co, the remark had been repeated and repeated, for finally it had been said and there was great relief that someone had been so tough, the Colonel had said, you just call me whenever you want a helicopter, Colonel Co, *you just call me*). Thuong had arrived, exactly to the minute. Anderson had halfway expected him to call the dinner off, but if anything Thuong appeared pleased with himself. It was as if he had scheduled both the battle and the dinner together. Anderson had first taken him around the Seminary, to the bar, introduced him to the other officers, and it was as if you could see the words freeze as they came out of the mouths of the Americans. The colder the words, the more polite Thuong was, deliberately lingering, in no hurry to leave. Finally they had left, at Anderson's urging, and Thuong had taken them to a different part of My Tho, far from the normal commercial side, to a tiny little restaurant with four tables and about six chairs.

There was no menu, no refrigeration, and several times throughout the evening the owner dispatched his son on a bicycle to a neighboring bar for ice cold beer. Thuong talked briefly with the owner, who appeared very proud to have the Lieutenant in his restaurant and proud to have Thuong too. The owner was contrite: there were no fresh shrimp, and shrimp were the specialty of the house, but he had been to the market that day and he had not liked the look of the shrimp. So they ate fish with a rich sauce and pork in thin strips, and a paste made out of dried shrimp and wound around a sugar cane stalk. It was an impressive meal, interrupted from time to time by the owner smacking his son if he found that their beer was running low. The conversation was even more difficult this time: Anderson had talked for more than thirty minutes about everything except Vietnam; finally he mentioned Vietnam and talked about everything but the battle. It was Thuong who interrupted him.

"But the battle, Lieutenant Anderson?" he asked.

And Anderson, poor, gentle Anderson, began by making excuses and implying the enemy force was larger than it was.

Thuong interrupted him and said: "Lieutenant Anderson, you are the most polite American I have ever seen, more polite even than the Vietnamese are supposed to be. When we are polite, we are not honest, and I think it is the same with you. It is not your great talent to be the liar, I think, and even your face is red. It was terrible, the battle, not even the snabu."

"The what?" Anderson asked.

"The snabu," Thuong said, "you know, what you call, I think, the fucking-up."

"The snafu," Anderson said.

They both laughed, tentatively.

"I am sorry," Thuong said. "It was not even the snafu. So I will be honest with you for the once and say what you know and that it was the great disgrace, and except for your American airplanes and American chopters, an even greater disgrace with hundreds more of the Vietnamese soldiers dead."

Anderson protested, somewhat feebly.

"No, no, you have been to the West Point, and I have not, not even Saint Cyr, or even the Vietnamese

Saint Cyr, but I know that it was a disgrace, and, Lieutenant, it was not our first, and it will not be our last. I wish I could tell you why it happens that way and that it will not happen again, but I cannot."

Anderson interrupted him to say that things were improving, the discipline was better, there were the helicopters, but Thuong looked at him, and smiled, a rare *friendly* smile, it was kindly.

"You came to save us, you Americans," he said.

"Not to save, to help," Anderson said.

"No, save, save is the better word, but I am afraid, Lieutenant, that you will find that we are not an easy people to save."

For once Anderson did not protest, and Thuong continued, his voice lower, his eyes almost closed, speaking as though he were talking to himself, "We cannot even save ourselves. That is the worst thing. We cannot save ourselves. I am sorry."

They ate in silence for a few minutes, and then Thuong, as though suddenly embarrassed, began to talk about himself, and to praise Anderson. He was a good soldier, a fine officer, if Thuong were Anderson's colonel, he would be proud to have a young officer like him; besides there would be jobs and countries ahead where people would be more grateful for his help; he was, after all, learning more lessons than he realized in Vietnam and what he was learning here, even the difficulties and the frustrations, would help him and he would be able to benefit from them. Someday he would be in another country and someone would ask him where he had served, he would answer Vietnam, and the other would say, "Ah, that is not only a brave man, but a patient one as well." They parted that night friends for the first time, with Thuong protesting strongly about the failure to eat fresh shrimp, and a promise that they would return again when the shrimp would be there to eat a happier meal.

But the promise was never fulfilled. Two days later, on another operation, Thuong had been nicer and gentler with him but no longer forthcoming. The ease of the previous evening was gone, and so too, soon was any benefit. It was as if Thuong were embarrassed by the weakness he had shown, and had retreated once more to his position of pride. The very fact that Anderson was such an excellent officer drove Thuong to a position of coolness and aloofness. Thuong was more aware of this than Anderson, aware of the fact that if Anderson were an inferior officer, if he were a Rainwater, then Thuong might be more pleasant to him, and that if Anderson weren't so nice, so constantly polite, Thuong might be more friendly to him. So they continued as uneasy counterparts and allies, Anderson working hard at the relationship. The harder he worked, the more aloof Thuong seemed to be, until Anderson himself would react and move back, show a coolness and occasionally become rude to Thuong. When this happened, Thuong would for a time become more pleasant with Anderson. Anderson belatedly in their relationship realized to a limited degree what was happening, but the other way was too much a part of him. He had been brought up a certain way to treat people in one manner, particularly people who were not so well off as he was. He could not, even for the sake of his job, even for the professionalism which he sought so much and wanted so badly, change twenty-five years of his background and upbringing. It was too high a price to pay; he was willing to pay with his life in this country, but he was unable to change this one weakness. He could not behave like a bastard with a yellow man in a poor country. So from time to time, largely because he could not control it, he would become angry and Thuong would react, but mostly he contented himself with fighting the struggle with kindness and losing with kindness.

So it was that they continued like two intimate strangers. There was no disagreement about the war, no lack of respect for each other's courage, and they had only one serious fight. It came when Anderson had been in the country three months, on a day of crushing heat, when an entire squad had passed out from heat exhaustion. They had gone through two villages, parched and barren at that time as if the very life had been baked out of them. The third village had seemed routine, perhaps a few more women in it, and they too seemed baked out. Anderson had sprawled out as quickly as he could under a tree, too tired to move, and had fallen into a stupor bordering on sleep. He had been disturbed by some noise from the center of the hamlet, but it had faded quickly. Then it began to ring in his ears and refused to go away, like an alarm clock that he did not want to answer. It remained so insistent that finally he began to listen. First there was male shrillness, with a sort of giggle; then a higher shrillness, probably female, sharper and a little louder; then a voice, clearly male, not so shrill, giggling a little more; then even more female shrillness with real anger, the voice higher and higher; then male again, shrill

no more, the giggle now a laugh, and then other
laughs; and then finally once more the other
voice, obviously female, now the pitch of a siren,
hysterical. He was fascinated so that even in the
heat he rose, stumbling at first, and walked toward the voices. There he found five women and
fifteen soldiers arguing and shouting. The soldiers all seemed to have ducks and some of the
women were fighting with them. One of the wom-
en still had her hands clasped to the neck of a
duck, and the duck was being stretched between
them. While they fought, she kicked, though at
close range, because the neck of the duck was so
short, and the soldier howled with laughter every
time she kicked. Anderson watched them for a
while, fascinated by the scene as all of it, detail by
detail (there were chickens as well as ducks), stamped
itself on his brain. It was widespread, not just one
woman, one duck, one soldier; it seemed his entire company was against the village, a small village (how many ducks could they have?). It was
widespread looting, nothing less, and Anderson
was furious; he did not realize that it had started
when the women had refused the soldiers water, a
mistake they would never make again, even on the
hottest of days. He watched in growing anger as
the soldiers laughed and began to play and mock
the women, Let's leave the ducks and take these
young girls, said one soldier. Then one of the
soldiers, seeing him there, not wanting him left
out, the troops after all liked the American advisers, walked over and offered Anderson one of his
two ducks, smiling conspiratorially at Anderson,
they were both in this together, there were enough ducks to

go around. Anderson declined the offer angrily and went to look for Thuong.

Thuong was at the far end of the village, which was unusual because normally he was in a position where he could watch the entire company; the significance of this, that Thuong had sensed something and wanted no part of it, did not strike Anderson until the next day. Thuong was very genial; he shifted in his place, making room for Anderson. He recalled Anderson's prediction made much earlier in the day about the heat ahead, when he Thuong had not sensed this. He recalled his own boyhood days when it was this hot, riding water buffaloes if you were lucky; he had loved water buffaloes in those days, and had ridden them without a thought of fear; now when he was older and stronger he was afraid of them. He talked and Anderson tried to break in, but Anderson, still true to his upbringing, was polite, and Thuong continued. Ah, the water buffaloes, when he was young they seemed so big that it was impossible since you were small to imagine anything that big could be stupid, but now he knew that size was not important, he knew how stupid these animals were. Anderson, bewildered by this man, usually so reticent, finally blurted out that there was a fight between the troops and the villagers. Thuong was surprised. His troops? His troops never stole. But Anderson insisted, good old American insistence, he had seen it, perhaps twenty ducks and chickens. Thuong smiled, a little indulgently this time; it wasn't possible, there weren't that many ducks in a hamlet like this. But, said Anderson, he had seen it. You are teasing me, said Thuong, you shouldn't tease a Vietnamese officer on a hot day. But Andersons insisted, the hands were on the ducks' necks, he had seen it.

Finally, Thuong, annoyed now, a look of irritation on his face, waited and then asked Anderson how many times a month he was paid. Once, said Anderson. When was that, Thuong said, still innocently. The first of the month. That was interesting, said Thuong, all armies are alike, are they not. It was the same for the troops here, though of course there were no checks here, even for officers. The trouble was, and Lieutenant Anderson must excuse him, because this had happened from time to time before, it was certainly not the proper way to run an army, and Thuong was the first to realize it, but what could he do, but it was a poor country, the trouble was, they had not been paid, and now it was the fifth of the month. Of course they could complain to the President, but that was not considered wise. So they are paying themselves, drawing their salaries. They are not really stealing chickens, Thuong said.

So there is really nothing I can do, he said, although I am sorry for the villagers.

Normally, Anderson would have taken it, as he had taken everything else. But he was angry and bitter, and the hot weather had affected him too.

"Sure," he said, "sure you're right, and I'm touched by the way you explain it. It makes it easy to understand. Only why don't you fight it? Fight Saigon. Fight Dang. Fight Co. But don't fight these poor damn people. Why don't you stop your troops, Lieutenant?"

"I am glad you care more about my people than I do, Lieutenant."

"And I am sorry I do."

With that they had walked away but it had gone very deep.

Thuong sensed the betrayal of the operation. He had more experience with it than the Americans. It had happened before to him in this war and when it had first happened, he had experienced anger and bitterness, but now he felt more fatigue than anger; it was the price of this war of Vietnamese against Vietnamese. The men on both sides, after all, looked the same, even to other Vietnamese, and it was not only impossible to tell in a man's eyes what cause his heart was committed to, but he had lost track of the morality; it was impossible also to say which was the higher purpose and the higher duty. They were now more blurred than before. When he was younger and it had first happened, he had felt a certain passion; someone was betraying not only himself but his colleagues and his men. He had gone back to Headquarters charged up, like a lawyer entering a courtroom. He came with facts, arguments, suspicions, and without doubts. He had his own suspect, a deputy officer in plans; had he not first called attention to the area and suggested the operation, was he not sullen and did he not seem to lack enthusiasm for the war, had he not been passed over and made to be disgruntled? And so Thuong privately made his suggestion, forgetting in the process those very qualities of his own which had placed him under so much suspicion, hindered his own career; in his anger he had become one of *them*. Then there had been a slip, and one of the government's agents had tipped them off by chance to the real betrayer, a young officer in the logistics section, a perfect officer, an upper class Catholic, enthusiastic without being aggressive, properly polite to all—even to Thuong, who was something of a rebel, the perfect agent, nothing wrong on the outside, the outside perfect, different only on the inside in the hatred for everything he had seen and known in his upbringing.

He was discovered and disposed of, and the other officer, to whom Thuong had confided his suspicions, asked him if he still thought of himself as a counter-intelligence agent, and for a time afterward referred to him as "Monsieur Deuxieme Bureau."

The experience had jolted Thuong; he had never again prejudged the suspect, and more important, he had learned to trust almost nobody. Of all operations Thuong distrusted provincial operations like this the most. He considered most of the province chiefs lazy and indifferent to their staffs; a little flattery to a superior and a younger officer was likely to be in a secure position forever. In addition, if something went wrong, as perhaps it was going wrong that day, it would be very hard for the Division to bring any pressure on the province chief. The province chief, no matter what happened today, would react and defend his own. It regarded the Division as virtually an enemy, and it was not about to lose face. So the province chief could call Saigon and tell the Presidency what had happened (it was the one thing in the province which always worked, the telephone line to the Presidency), and before nightfall the Presidency would call Co. The voice would be sharp and stern and brief. Co must tend to the

Division and stay out of the business of the province chief; he was not to enter into politics, he was to fight the war. Their one victory out of this would be that they need not go on a provincial operation again for about six months. They could abstain and the province chief would be wary of calling Saigon (if he called, the Presidency would tell him to stay in his province and attend to politics and not try and run the army); then in the seventh month they would both have to confer on an operation for fear the other would complain to Saigon. They would schedule an operation and he, Thuong, and all the other little Thuongs, would go ahead and walk through some operation, not knowing whose hands it had gone through, not knowing if someone were sitting back and watching them (a year earlier in the Twenty-first Division, they had captured a Vietcong after-action report of a betrayed operation in which the VC, alerted beforehand to the government's moves, had complained about the tardiness of the Arvin to arrive at a certain checkpoint, and cited poor leadership as the reason).

Thuong had once complained about these provincial operations to Chinh who was the commander of the battalion now on the East Wing.

"What are you complaining about?" said Chinh.

"These betrayals," said Thuong.

"Betrayals," said Chinh. "Why worry. It happens once a year, twice a year. Not very often. What do you expect, Thuong, perfection? Do you expect our officers not to talk. They are Vietnamese like you and me. Maybe it's me who's tipped it off, by being so pleased with the idea of an operation that I make love to my wife too many times, and so the houseboy knows and perhaps he is a Vietcong. But I cannot kill the houseboy and I cannot stop making love to the wife, so the only answer is to kill more Vietcong. It is foolish to talk about betrayal."

So Thuong walked among the troops trying to make them more alert, trying to make them sharper in the deadening heat.

"They got twenty out of your sister company," he said, as he moved among them. "Would you like me to pick twenty out of this company for them? I can tell you which twenty, the lazy and stupid ones. You, you, and you. Do you want to die here today, die on such a hot day, or do you want to go back to your women as heroes?"

"The women already know we are heroes," said one of them.

"The women are smarter than you think. They come to me and they say how can Private Thuan be such a hero as he claims when he is so weak and lazy at home. They want me to explain to them," Thuong said.

Chapter Six

AT NOON they stopped for lunch just outside their second village, Ap Thanh; it had been one of the smaller victories of Beaupre and Anderson that they had convinced Dang to keep the troops out of villages at lunchtime; otherwise the village inevitably supplied the menu. Beaupre had two sandwiches, thick slabs of ham prepared by the mess sergeant (in the beginning when he had come to them, the bread was always soaking wet; so the next time he would place them higher on his body to keep them dry, and, of course, they would still be wet; now he wrapped them and sealed them in a plastic wrapper). They were dry, but they looked so heavy and in the heat he could not bear the thought of eating, and he put them aside. Dang offered him some rice, and at first he turned it down, but Dang was insistent. It was not the day to eat American food, it was the day to eat Vietnamese food. Dang would not eat rice if he were in the north of Beaupre's country, and so Beaupre relented and gratefully began to eat a little rice and then a little more; then Dang offered him a simple soup broth and he drank that, and was revived slightly.

"Our American warrior, Beaupre, will make a good Vietnamese soldier before he leaves," said Dang, and Beaupre smiled, and promised to take Dang skiing in Vermont when he came to America, and they would eat ham instead of rice.

"The Captain Beaupre is a skier?" Dang asked.

No, said Beaupre, he came from a part of the country where it was hot and there was never any snow; he had never learned to ski.

"Never ski, so you are really like the Vietnamese captain who do not ski, either," said Dang, "and you make the jokes with the Captain Dang, ha-ha."

After lunch Beaupre stood up and walked around, checking on the unit; the heavy weapons were pointed in and security was minimal. By all odds it was stupid soldiering, but it was also true that the Vietcong were very unlikely to charge a government position during daytime, even a government lunchroom. Instead they would wait, concealed and ready in carefully prepared positions, and let the government come to them, let the Arvin stand in the open. Beaupre was afraid to sit down and rest, afraid he might pass out again and knowing that if he did, Anderson would have to turn him in. So he settled for half best; he leaned against a tree and smoked a cigarette, and played for an instant with the idea of both Dang and himself skiing in Vermont, *"Ah, it is my good friend the Vietnamese skier, Captain Dang, Captain you are doing too much better than I am and I am losing face,"* as he pulled Dang out of a snowdrift.

This particular reverie was shattered by Anderson who came up with the radio.

"They have our goddamn number today," he said. "Raulston and the thirteenth battalion just got hit. Few minutes ago. Bad. Damn bad. Heavy losses. Very heavy. They thought Raulston bought it at first, but they found him later, hit in the leg; they think maybe the VC went right past him and left him for dead. Raulston kept mumbling, 'Everybody dead, everybody dead.' He's close to it. Lot of dead. Worse than the first one. Same goddamn business. They were caught in the open paddy field. They were halfway across the paddy, and almost through when the VC opened up. Maybe half the battalion was wiped out. Hell of a cross fire. Each time they identified a machine gun, and started to work on it, another one would open up. Goddamn VC knew everything they were going to do. They got the Arvin battalion commander Chinh, that good one. He was at the head of the column when they got hit, and he didn't mess around. Took a flanking party and tried to sweep the VC, and they set out, him right at the head, and the VC waiting for them, and gunned the entire flanking party down. Badly torn up. Bad. So they got both the rear and the front of the column. Body of this Chinh ain't nothing but torn up. About the time they got his body, the Colonel was yelling for them to send in a flanking party and to get someone to lead it, and they told him that it was already out and already torn up. So he wanted to know who was leading it, and they told him it was Chinh and he's very impressed. It's bad over there, the CP says. They got one medevac chopper in there now, and another one is down. Three dead in one of the choppers, and the other chopper boys are pissed off to beat hell. They say it's all rigged against them. CP says he's never seen the chopper boys so angry. CP says they're moving the reserve force in, though Co didn't want to, and the Vietnamese are so nervous that they've landed the reserves far enough back from the tree line that they won't draw any fire, probably won't reach the tree line for another hour. Said the Colonel's pissed off and in a rage and frightened too. Says it's the first time he's seen any fear in him. Bad day. Thinks even the Colonel wasn't unhappy about landing the reserve force."

"What does the Colonel think?" Beaupre asked.

"The Colonel doesn't like it one damn bit. They're trying to decide now whether to abort or not, and just pick you boys up and let you sleep the rest of it off. But I think they're afraid to mention it to the friendlies because the friendlies would think they're chickening out. So you may have to keep walking. Sorry. Give my best to the friendlies."

It was what happened to the flanking party which removed any of Beaupre's remaining doubts. It was all too well done, too professional. It was an eerie feeling as if the VC were playing games with him. He saw himself as a blip on someone else's radar scope; they were watching his every move, and waiting for him, in their own good time and good place. He knew with a terrible certainty that they were going to be ambushed. The VC were probably picking out, he thought, the particular part of his anatomy where they would get him arguing among themselves for the choicest part. The Vietcong knew everything about the operation; they had, he thought, probably drawn the damn thing up for us.

He looked at the map and calculated the distances and the times of the ambushes: eleven-forty-five and twelve-thirty. He looked at the route ahead alongside the canal. About one-fifteen they would enter their second village, Ap Thanh, on their way to the final linkup, a linkup which would probably never take place now. He looked at the map some more and he decided that the ambush would come after the village; the VC would wait, and the Arvin would come into the village tense and nervous and ready and the VC would not be there, and so the Arvin would become careless and sloppy again, and then right after the village, hit them. He took the map and showed Anderson where he thought it would happen.

"The party will be right there. The first place where there's a good open shot at us."

There was, he showed Anderson, a smaller canal a little more than a quarter of a mile from the main canal, running parallel to it. They had to get off the main canal; the party was waiting for them on the big canal, he was sure of that. It was a terrible thing to do; in any other war if you were that sure of an ambush, you could flank it and then bait it; but that would be too much here, the troops weren't good enough. Now the only important thing to do was avoid contact with the heart of the ambush. They had to get off the main canal.

He went back on the radio and said very clearly and slowly, spacing his words carefully: "Tell the Colonel that we are going ahead just like he wanted. Straight ahead. Tell him I don't like the idea of going back or detouring."

He repeated the message nice and slowly, "We don't want to detour or abort. We don't think there's anything to worry about."

The CP, somewhat confused, said sure, he would pass the message on, if that was what Beaupre really wanted.

Then Beaupre told Anderson, "You get your young friend there, and make sure he passes the same message on their radio, the exact same message, and make sure he repeats it a couple of times. Shouldn't be any problem getting them to repeat it. Tell that fella he doesn't have to talk to Dang about it. Tell him not to clear it with Dang, but to make sure it gets out. Tell him I'll work on our friend Dang."

"The warrior Dang?"

"Yeah, that's the one."

Anderson started to walk away.

"And tell your Vietnamese friend to start checking out some of those people back at his headquarters and find out who they really love," Beaupre said.

Beaupre went to find Dang. The troops were moving again, and he had to make his way back through the column. They were bunched up and chattering, and he thought of the open field ahead which the Vietcong had prepared for them, and he thought what a goddamn silly business to die here, surrounded by soldiers like this as if it were really a great joke, not even a war, to walk laughing into the ambush. He was frightened now; until now this war had too often made him sloppy and lazy, even arrogant. He had been contemptuous of his colleagues, his allies, the people, even from time to time, the enemy. It was he who had told the chaplain the men were not frightened enough to pray. But now he cared, and he did not want to die; he did not want to be among the laughing ten pins.

"Captain Dang," he said, "this has not been a good day."

Dang smiled and said yes, and praised him for being revived by the Vietnamese soup. "You see how Vietnamese you have become. By the time you leave here, you will speak Vietnamese and you will take the *nuoc mam* back to the America with you."

"No," said Beaupre, thinking to himself, I must do this properly; if I never do anything again properly, I must do this right. I must be careful. I must not antagonize this little bastard. I must talk to him like I love him. I love him.

"There have been two other wings of this operation, and there have been two ambushes already. We are the third wing."

"There has been a battle, two battles. Many Communist Vietcong have been killed. Many, many Vietcongs."

"In America we call this a pattern. A dangerous one." If I think he is a great man, perhaps it will show in my face. He is a great man. I am sure of it now, a great man.

"If the Communists come after me, there will be many more dead, I promise that."

A great man, Beaupre thought, he is a great man.

"Captain," he said, "I have an idea. It really goes back to something you taught me when I first came to your country and you were explaining guerrilla war and the enemy to me." And he talked and hoped the Captain would listen, a great man, he reminded himself as he began.

He finished and he walked away from Dang. He wondered, not for the first time, what it would be like to be an adviser to the VC. All the advisers thought about it. Just for a week, he thought, even if it meant wearing black pajamas and walking all night. Not so much grinning, he thought, he was sure the VC were sterner and never grinned. Their weapons would be clean. Dang would be on the other side. There was a quality of luxury to his thoughts.

After the first ambush Thuong had not been bitter—irritated, and perhaps even a little bit bored by Anderson; after all, every time there was an American death, Thuong did not go up to Anderson and express condolences for some sergeant, some heavy, fat sergeant, who had come over here to sleep with Vietnamese whores. But after the second ambush, he was bitter and angry. Chinh had been killed leading a flanking party and Chinh was one of the few officers in the entire division that Thuong both admired and trusted, a thin muscled little man from the north, looking in his uniform like someone's younger brother, smaller than all the other officers, wearing his hair very long, deliberately, Thuong was sure, because the style of the others was to wear it short and cropped like the Americans. A fine soldier, admired by his men and his contemporaries. Thuong envied Chinh his hatred for the Vietcong; Chinh did not talk about it but Thuong assumed it was something to do with the north, the death of a father or a mother, perhaps only an uncle. But in addition to that complete and simple and almost gentle bravery, he was a genuinely good and trusted friend, a man with an uncommon sense of humor which slipped out from time to time when they were among close friends. Chinh did a great variety of imitations, impeded in seeking new ones because the old ones were so popular and were always requested: a French officer waxing his mustache in front of an imaginary mirror, trying to get the mustache to the right point of arrogance, then taking his beret, working on that for several minutes in order to get the right angle, the angle which would show that he had killed many men and loved many women, then finally gaining the angle, smiling and winking at himself, and blowing the mirror a kiss and going off to war. Then a Vietcong officer giving a course in political instruction, very solemn and serious, making sure that no one slept during the lesson, which was a class on How to Love and Emulate Ho Chi Minh's beard, the pointer flicking back and forth to the imaginary blackboard, while the instructor pointed out strand after strand in the beard, giving authorized lengths for every hair, decreeing that no one could have a longer beard than Ho but that uniformed soldiers' must be an inch and a half shorter and that political cadremen could not wear them at all since it was well known that the

Americans suspected anyone with a beard; then the Commissar, finishing the class and before starting the next lesson, which was on food discipline, slipping away and greedily stuffing food into his mouth. Then Ngo Dinh Diem, reviewing the local Cong Hoa youth parade, the province chief giving the great Fascist salute, but Diem, absentmindedly, and a little dazed from the heat, losing his bearings, turning around, forgetting that he had completed the review, and the province chief, relaxed and rather sloppy after being told by a Diem aide that his salute was the best of the week, rushing to snap to attention again, and then Diem forgetting once more and the whole process repeated once more. Finally an imitation on how to love your American counterpart, in which Chinh did a series of reverse imitations of Raulston, first putting his arm around the American's back each morning and slapping him on the back, feeling his arm muscle, and expressing great delight and surprise at the size of it, then opening his wallet and bringing out photographs of his family and showing them to Raulston, winking at the audience and saying, *Americans love children, it's a good way to win them over,* and then suggesting to Raulston that they might change dollars; he had even learned some of Raulston's vocabulary and kept referring to him as "old American buddy," which delighted his friends, "old American buddy, let's us change some old U.S. dollars for some Vietnamese piastres or disasters, huh old buddy."

The Americans, Thuong thought, would say what a tough little bastard Chinh was, and he cursed the Americans, remembering as he did, what Chinh had said: you are too hard on them, my young friend, it is the trouble with all you intellectuals, at which point Thuong had protested angrily about the word intellectual, but Chinh had brushed him aside—you are too hard on them because you do not disagree with the way they fight, in fact you admire that, but you disagree with why they are fighting. You think it is pointless for people to fight so well for so little, but you are too hard, that is their business. They are nice people. They are brave although their food is bad, and their cigarettes are for women. So what. I know you, Thuong; if they fought not so well, you would probably like them more. It is fortunate for us that we are not all intellectuals like you.

Thuong walked among the troops, telling them not to sleep today. They could sleep the next time out, telling them he had made a secret agreement with the VC to ambush only the lazy ones, the ones who slept in the field. As they approached Ap Thanh, he told the advance elements to recon with fire and he ordered them to fan out, telling them that he was tired of carrying five bodies off the field instead of one, that he was likely to pull a back muscle if they weren't more careful. Beaupre heard the order come back up to the point and was pleased; even though he was sure in his own mind there were no troops in the village, he was certain that the noise would be heard by some of the VC and would convince them that the Arvin were falling into the baited trap.

The noise as they approached the village was terrifying: light machine guns going off, even the occasional thump of a mortar. Anderson, at the back of the column and moving now to his right and toward the open field in front of the village, was not sure what was happening or why it was happening. He had not heard the order to recon with fire; it had gone up the file, but not down, and he cursed the Vietnamese for not passing on intelligence. He was sure they knew something he did not know. He saw the soldier next to him firing a grease gun, and he quickly fired half a clip from his weapon toward a bush. He heard some moans from behind him and began to crawl forward. It was damn stupid of the Viets not to let him know what was going on there, he thought, and damn typical. The firing was very intense, but he could not tell exactly where it was coming from: usually he could—could sense the pockets of the enemy and see the flashes of firing—but this time he scanned the tree line without success. He felt frustrated.

It was like a terrible storm; it threatened to go on forever, building in intensity, and then, almost without warning, turned to half power, and almost before that change could register, it was only a trickle and it was over. By the time Anderson reached the village, the first patrol was inside; the troops were laughing and joking among themselves and at first Anderson was puzzled, not realizing what had happened, and then finally it struck him that it had only been a reconnaissance, and he felt foolish and angry at the Viets. No one ever tells you anything in this country, he thought. He looked at them, half expecting them to laugh at him, and then he realized that they were not aware of his anger and foolishness, that if they had seen him during those minutes, they assumed he too was firing as they were, that he was not in battle, that he had not dodged bullets. He felt his anger slip away and he remembered that he liked these people. He smiled at them.

"How many men did we lose taking the village?" he said. "It was a great battle," and they all laughed with him.

Ap Thanh was a tiny village, the kind the Colonel frequently said showed on Vietcong maps but not on their own. But it had a quality even beyond that. Beaupre was struck by how much it reminded him of a ghost town, but not even a real ghost town, instead, a cardboard one set up by a movie company. It was smaller than any village he had seen in Vietnam, with only a few huts, and they appeared to have been deserted long ago. It was completely silent, not just in contrast with the barrage of a few minutes ago, but silent in itself. Even Beaupre, who liked to regard all Vietnamese people and all Vietnamese villages as being alike, was touched by it; he had seen almost everything else in this country but he had never seen this. He asked Dang what had happened to the welcoming committee, but Dang did not see the humor and told him that the Communist Vietcong was responsible for this.

"Most likely a massacre, Captain Dang," Beaupre said, picking him up.

"Yes," said Dang, "that is the word, massacre. From your Indian films." He seemed quite pleased with himself.

Beaupre watched Anderson talking with the young Vietnamese lieutenant, probably, he thought, asking where the people were, and felt for a moment a rare bit of sympathy for the Vietnamese people. Beaupre felt a little better now, well enough to risk sitting down, and he moved to the shade, but that did not help him to escape the heat. The sweat seemed to pour out even more freely now that he had stopped walking. He thought perhaps when he finished this operation, if he did, he would go easier on drinking. There was no point in it, he was sure he could go lighter, he would let someone else close up the bar. He was sitting there rolling water around in his mouth but not drinking it, he was proud of that, when they found the old man.

Beaupre had seen many old men in Vietnam before, withered and thin, but this old man was the frailest and most withered he had ever seen. In a very white pajama suit, Beaupre noticed, whoever that old son of a bitch is, he still has someone to do his laundry. They had found him by accident in one of the huts; they had searched the hut once earlier, but he had been so thin and still that they had not noticed him. Beaupre, hearing the explanation, could believe it.

They surrounded him but did not search him. Dang decided to do the interrogating. Anderson was there, and Beaupre, intrigued, moved over and signaled to Anderson that he wanted a running translation. Anderson nodded.

Dang said something. "Dang's asking where all the people are," Anderson whispered, and the old man looked at Dang, looked up and down the village.

"The people are all gone," he said. It was said as fact. It was indisputable. For a moment Dang said nothing.

Then Dang said something else, a number of things quickly in a row: where have the people gone, what have you done with them, where is the enemy, have you helped the enemy. For a moment the old man said nothing. Then he said something very slowly and proudly. Beaupre saw the looks of surprise on the faces of the Vietnamese before he heard Anderson's words: "He says that he's never done anything to help the French, he says he never told them anything."

They were all astounded. Even Beaupre was stunned. "Sonofabitch," he said, "what's Dang going to say now?"

He saw a tiny smile appear on the face of the young Vietnamese lieutenant; the others, if they found it funny were controlling their smiles. From reading their faces the old man might have been reciting a pledge of allegiance to the government. The old man said something more: "The French tried, but he never talked," and Anderson said, "He did not let the French fool him."

"Dang's telling him that it's all right, that the old war is over and the French have all gone," Anderson said.

The old man began to talk again. "The old guy is saying that he never helped them, and there's people here who'll swear to it, that his loyalty is known, and he's glad they've gone. But he wants to know why everybody's here if the French are gone. Now Dang's saying there's a new enemy even worse than the French. The old man wants to know if they speak strange languages like the French. Dang's pretty annoyed and a little pissed off. He says yes, they speak funny and strange languages. The old guy says in that case he won't help them either, that he never helped the French, the French came and asked him a lot of questions, and he told them a lot of lies ["I believe that," Beaupre interjected. "That's the first thing all day I believe"], and the next time the French came he sent them to a place where soldiers just like us killed some of them. He says the next day the French came back and killed a lot of people including his wife and son, and he was hiding or they would have killed him, so he certainly wouldn't help them after that, and now he's very glad they're gone, he never liked the sound of their language. The old guy doesn't seem to like Dang too awfully much. He just asked Dang if he fought against the French. Dang's saying of course he did, everybody did."

Almost instantly, perhaps because of the last question, Dang broke the conversation off. But now the old man wanted to talk: he was glad to welcome people like Dang here, Dang must have tea with him, a man who has killed as many Frenchmen as Dang must pay him honor to share tea. Dang, irritated, said no, they had work ahead of them. Ah, many of this new enemy to kill, said the old man, this new enemy with the strange language. The old man seemed to wink at Dang; and Dang said yes, that was it, they would come back another time to drink the tea. Beaupre had been amused by the entire conversation at first, but he was a little worried now, afraid that it would embarrass Dang and make it more difficult for him to take the slight detour Beaupre wanted.

Chapter Seven

THEY WERE ABOUT to leave the village when Dang sought Beaupre out. "I have decided to play games with the Communist Vietcong," he said. "We will set a trap for him."

Beaupre listened; he suspected that this meant Dang had decided to follow his advice, to swing the main party off the prescribed route to a subsidiary canal at the last minute and to send a recon element along the main route.

"I have decided we will go here," said Dang, pointing to the subsidiary canal, parallel and less than a half mile from the main canal. "Then if the Communist Vietcong are on the Dong Thien canal, they will attack our patrol, and we will swing around and [there was a pause] I will destroy him." He banged his fist into his hand. "If he is along the smaller canal, I will destroy him there too."

You miserable little sonofabitch, Beaupre thought, and smiled, relieved, his hand reaching up to touch Dang's shoulder. He praised the plan, it was typical, he said, of the many things that Captain Dang had taught him about this war. The enemy would be off balance, thanks to Captain Dang, and the enemy would pay for this. *You miserable little sonofabitch,* he thought.

Then they began to work out details of the plan. The decoy patrol would have eight men, and at least one automatic weapon. They would make as much noise as possible, they would carry transistor radios and play them and they could talk in the ranks. They would file out of Ap Thanh along with the rest of the unit, but once outside, the rest of the unit would slip off and make the detour, and the recon patrol would keep going straight down the main canal. It was not a bad plan, and they agreed quickly; but later as they were breaking from the village, Beaupre checked the weapons of the recon patrol. My God, he thought, they're as happy and unperturbed as if they were going to Saigon on a weekend pass. He looked at them and wondered if he would ever understand these people; he knew that American troops would be tense and bitter in a situation like this; he was not sure if it were American troops he would even dare to have a decoy patrol. He found only carbines and M-1s.

"Captain, there seems to be some mistake," Beaupre told Dang. "There is no automatic weapon among the recon patrol."

"I do not think there is any mistake, Captain Bopay," Dang said. "I do not think there will be any problem."

"But these men may need an automatic weapon. If they get ambushed, they'll need time until you can swing around and reach them, Captain Dang. I know you'll be coming very fast, but they'll need help."

"I do not think they will have any trouble with the Communist Vietcong," Dang said. "I do not think any mistake has been made. Perhaps you do not understand."

Oh, I understand all right, Beaupre thought, I've been in this country long enough and that's one of the things I've learned to understand. Saigon would not like losing a BAR; it was one thing an officer could not lie about; he could lie about the number of dead troops but not an automatic weapon. He looked at Dang for a long minute and felt a little sick, and for a brief moment he wished he had not thought of the detours and decoys.

In each of his different wars Beaupre had always had visions of death, but they had all been quite different and separate. In World War II the vision had been of a shell, a giant shell from a tank or cannon coming on him before he could hear it, so there was no real listening for it, with only enough noise in the final split second to confirm all his fears, splashing his body in all different directions, his arms and legs coming off, his body scrambled. In Korea the vision had differed. It was more theatrical, crossing the lines, and then betrayed by a double agent, captured in some freezing little hut, then two days of questioning without food so that his strength ebbed by the minute in the cold, until finally it didn't matter or not whether he lived; and a bullet in the head, no one to rescue him because no one even knew that he needed to be rescued. In Vietnam it had been different, an idea less persistent because the thought of death had not been so persistent. He was not pursued by it here as he had been in Korea, here it was more creative, the idea evolving slowly, sniper bullet, just one—a chance bullet really because they were such bad shots—then dying slowly and warmly for a period of an hour because no one could get him to a medic, a process made all the more terrible, the very slowness of it, by his ability to study and watch and record his own death. The whole thing would be judged a mistake later, would be doubly regretted, that the sniper had actually hit him, that the medic had not arrived, for afterward the wound would be judged an easy one to treat, it would all be a mistake. His death would be more cause for cursing the impotence of the country. Others would do the cursing.

He was on the radio now, talking carefully in their code, asking for air support to be ready. The CP was obviously amused, and the surprise came over the radio. Beaupre, after all, was the leading Air Force baiter at the bar, he hated the Air Force, mocked the zoomies, they were clean sheets men, he referred to them as the movie stars; they had, he would say, his voice mocking, the handsomest colonels and generals of any branch of service, even better-looking than the Marines, their generals looked like lieutenants with gray sprinkled in their hair, their skins still soft and young. Over the radio he could hear the CP's surprise and amusement, *you* want the *zoomies*. Through the code Beaupre was able to tell that the T-28s were not ready at the moment. "Tomorrow isn't good enough," Beaupre said.

"You're not the only one we've got," the CP said. "You haven't even been shot at."

"We're about to have that remedied," Beaupre said.

"I can't promise anything," said the CP.

"Try for before nightfall," said Beaupre. "For old times' sake."

"Look," said the CP, "you don't have cause to talk like that with me. It isn't my fault. I don't do the requisitioning around here. I had 'em, you'd get them, but I don't have them. I'm doing the best I can. Soon as I get 'em, you'll be the first to know. Can't give you what I don't have. It's not so easy being here. You think you have all the problems."

"That's right," said Beaupre, "I think I have all the problems."

Beaupre turned back to the troops: they were moving well, and they were keeping the silence demanded of them; for once he was relatively pleased with them. For once they seemed serious. Maybe they were thinking about death as much as he was; maybe they didn't want to die any more than he did. He was near the point, and he was nervous as they moved into relatively open country.

The first burst hit behind Beaupre and killed fifteen men. The first thing Beaupre knew was that it had happened, and then that he was still alive. He heard screams from behind him and then another burst, this one very long as if the gunner's finger had gotten stuck on the trigger and he couldn't stop. Beaupre was down, not returning the fire, simply down and alive and trying to find out what had happened, trying to catch his breath and trying to stay alive. It had happened so quickly, even though he knew it might happen and had almost expected it, that he did not even remember what the scene had looked like before the burst. They had been moving along the canal, and were still short of a junction. There was some thick foliage to the right of them and the canal was to the left. He looked behind him and could tell from the way the bodies were sprawled out that there were a lot of dead. The other troops, the living, seemed hopelessly disorganized, and he wondered why there seemed to be so much confusion. Why wasn't someone in charge, he thought. Someone should be in charge. He looked at the way the troops were sprawled out and decided the VC must have hit the midsection of the column and not the point because they wanted a government officer and Arvin officers were rarely at the point. Because of that, he was alive.

The main weapon, or at least what seemed to be the main weapon, opened up again. It was to the left, on the other side of the canal, perhaps fifty yards away, perhaps closer. There was still no answering fire. He looked further down the column and realized that there must have been two simultaneous bursts. There was a second pocket of sprawled bodies, and Beaupre had the terrible feeling one of them was an American.

His first job was to mark the weapons. One he was sure now was a light machine gun. He listened to see if there were another machine gun, and finally decided it was a BAR up ahead of him somewhere. The machine gunner was firing off long bursts and Beaupre's first reaction was that it was unusual for them to throw ammo around like that, they must be cocky. Usually they were like instructors at the range, firing off short bursts, never wasting ammunition.

Behind him the Vietnamese were simply lying down. They were also, he realized, looking at him as if it were for him to tell them where and when they would die, right there where they lay or perhaps a few yards forward, right now or in ten minutes. He sensed somehow that he was now the unofficial commander; he did not know whether Dang was dead or not, but it probably made little difference. Dang could give no commands now. He crawled a few yards toward better cover, took a grenade, pulled the pin and threw it. It fell on the other side of the canal, hopelessly short, but at least it was fire returned. He took his Armalite, aimed it where the light machine gun was and fired off his own short burst, then slipped back to better cover. An answering burst, much longer, much surer, than his, came right back. He felt that the Viets were still watching him and waiting. He wanted to yell at them to fire, but he did not know the Vietnamese word for fire. Perhaps if he fought, they would finally, reluctantly, fight too. Behind him he could still hear the sounds of the Viets dying, though the sounds were lower and softer by the minute. When he first came to the country, he had been told the Vietnamese were not like Americans, they died silently, but it was wrong, they died like everyone else. He could not see Dang or the young Vietnamese lieutenant, but he was sure that the silence confirmed Anderson's death. Anderson, if nothing else, was ferociously aggressive; he would have emptied several clips by now, he would be rallying troops, his voice, that voice so distinctly West Point even when he spoke Vietnamese, would have been loud and clear. Beaupre fired another burst and signaled to one of the Viets behind him with a grease gun to come forward. He noticed that even though they were hugging the ground and not firing, they were watching him intently. They want to live too, we all want to live, he thought, and they will do what I want. Miraculously the Viet crawled forward. There was a long burst from the side machine gun, but it fell short.

He did not speak the language so he used his hands. He signaled to the soldier that he wanted to talk with Captain Dang, that he would return— that was the important part, that he would return— but that the Viet must keep firing until he got back. He caught the eye of another one, motioned him to a tree a few yards back and told him to fire. He used his hands, and when the Viet took up a position, Beaupre nodded his approval, and the Viet grinned. Good God, Beaupre thought, they grin even here. The Viet began to fire. Beaupre started to crawl back and again, a miracle, both Vietnamese began to cover him. He moved back conscious of his own fear, and strangely enough, his sanity. He sensed for the first time that because the VC had taken such good cover on the other side of the canal they lacked the elevation for their field of fire, and therefore it was possible to crawl. They had made that one mistake. God bless, he thought, they were not perfect, they were like us too, they did not want to die.

He heard the exchange of fire as he moved

back and reached the site of the first burst. There was a trail of dead Vietnamese. They were scattered in all directions, as if someone with a giant hand had rolled them out like dice. He realized that he did not recognize them or know their names. One of them had been sucking on a sugar cane stalk and the cane was still in his mouth. Beside him was another man with part of his face shot away, he had been caught in the chin and neck. The first burst, Beaupre thought, had obviously been a little high or it might have been worse. Another lay toppled over on his side, with his palm outstretched as if he had been praying; another lay sprawled down, his eyes closed, completely silent, but his transistor radio on, either he had switched it on when he was dying, or else he had violated the noise blackout, the radio was playing their damn singsong music. Beaupre saw a tiny little man with a BAR lying next to him—they always gave the biggest weapons to their smallest people— and wrestled the weapon out of his hands and continued to crawl. He saw three Viets still alive, not even holding their weapons, their faces turned away from the enemy. He motioned for them to fire, but they were not ready. He cursed them bitterly, racially, *fight, you goddamn gooks*, he said. They refused to understand or heed his curses. He crawled toward one, grabbed a weapon, and jammed the stump of it into the man's stomach. The soldier reluctantly accepted the weapon, and then the others too, slowly, so very slowly, moved to pick up their weapons. He turned and fired a burst himself, received another in return, and then finally the three soldiers began to fire.

He went further back. He could see Anderson

now. He had been hit and spun around, and was lying face to the sky with his mouth still open. He had been hit in the neck and chest. Beaupre looked for Captain Dang but could not see him. Goddamn, he thought, he was supposed to be here near the center. He looked again, finally spotting Dang a few yards away, apparently hit in the legs but quite obviously suffering more from shock, sitting there motionless. Beaupre suddenly needed the young Vietnamese lieutenant, Thuong, that was his name. He looked around and cursed the Lieutenant. Bugged out too, not surprising, they all do. He decided to wait there a minute or two, and then if necessary, go after him. Just then he saw Thuong moving slowly toward him.

He told Thuong that Anderson was dead. "Captain Dang is as good as dead, too," he added.

The Lieutenant said gently that Captain Dang had been fighting the war for a long time. The response coming then, so soft, with both of them under fire and flattened out on the ground, moved him.

The Lieutenant added, "I am sorry, Captain, but I do not think there will be any help for us." Beaupre took Anderson's radio and called the CP. The CP had already heard reports of the ambush from the Viets and had assumed that both Anderson and Beaupre were dead.

"I'm still alive," said Beaupre.

"We're all damn glad about that," the CP said. "You stay in there, hear, we'll get some help to you soon."

"What can you give me right now? We need it now!" said Beaupre.

"The choppers went back to Soc Trang thirty

minutes ago," the CP said. "There isn't much chance of their coming back. Most of the reserve force is already committed and Co is afraid of an even bigger ambush. He's very edgy," the CP said.

"Stuff Co," Beaupre said.

"How big is it?" asked the CP.

"I don't know," Beaupre said. "Yes, it's big, I'm big. For God's sake, can't you send me something? What about the T-28s?"

The CP said that one of them had engine trouble so they both had gone back to Bien Hoa.

"Send one of them," Beaupre said.

"They like to fly in pairs," the CP said. "They don't like it alone. Air Force is touchy about that."

"I'm touchy, too," Beaupre said.

There was a moment of silence, and then the CP asked: "You going to make it?"

"I'll let you know later," Beaupre said.

"Look," the CP said, "if I said anything earlier too smart, I'm sorry, I didn't mean it. I know how it is out there. Okay?"

"Okay," said Beaupre, "I know." Jesus, he thought, they must really be giving me up; doesn't want any angry words hanging on his conscience.

Beaupre listened for a moment and heard only the sounds of Communist automatic weapons. *Tell them to return the goddamn fire,* he screamed at the Lieutenant. *Can't you make them do even that? What the hell kind of people are they?* He might be wrong, but he thought he detected a look of sympathy on the Lieutenant's face; perhaps his own fear showed too clearly.

"I don't want to die here either, Captain," said the Lieutenant.

*   *   *

Thuong had been near the tail end of the column when the ambush began. He rolled over behind a clump of trees not knowing at first whether or not it was cover, but wanting to get down, not knowing where the fire was coming from. He sensed that the attack was coming from the front of the column, and so he slowly began to work his way toward its head. He came by the radio man. The radio was still on but the operator was slumped down. Thuong crawled to it, picked it up, and moved to his left toward cover as a burst came near.

"We are hit, we are hit," he said.

"Are you sure?" the Headquarters said.

"Yes," he said, his voice calm, "I am sure. We are hit, heavy casualties."

His voice sounded too calm and almost indifferent. The CP did not recognize it, for he rarely went on the radio himself.

"Where is Nguyen?" Headquarters asked, giving the name of the radio man.

"Nguyen is dead," he answered, perhaps lying, because he had not even checked the pulse.

The radio came back with a coded password which confused Thuong at first. He did not use the radio often and he had forgotten the password; finally he remembered, gave it, and told the Headquarters: "We are not VC. We are not VC, but we are hit."

"We wanted to be sure," the Headquarters said.

Then Headquarters excused itself for a moment, came back and said that Co and the province chief said they could do nothing for them, they must stay in there, that the Americans had foolishly sent the helicopters back and the American fighter planes weren't working as usual. They must stay there and perhaps something would develop. Would they like some artillery? The province chief had checked and they were within artillery range.

"No," said Thuong, even more terrified, "no artillery, not now, thank the province chief." The province chief, he thought, loves to bombard the entire countryside with artillery, and we are not dug in, and the VC are.

"Yes," said the CP, and excused himself again. Then he returned: the Lieutenant was to give the province chief's warm regards and personal admiration to Captain Dang, and to remind him that they had lots of artillery.

"Fine," said Thuong. He put another man on the radio, and then slipped out to the back of the column. The firing was still very heavy but it was not coming from the rear and that made him nervous. He took two men who were doing nothing—that was easy, they were all doing nothing—one with a grease gun, and one with a carbine, and took them to the very end of the column, and told them not to let anyone slip up on them. He didn't care what happened at the front of the column, they were not to turn around. Those were their orders, if they were stabbed to death from behind, he, Thuong, would take the responsibility and they would both be Heroes of the Republic if there were anyone left alive to recommend them. They both nodded; he was sure they would fight well in defense, or at least if there were a rush from the rear. The rest of the column would have a few minutes of warning.

The rear taken care of, he started to work his way back to the center of the column.

He was surprised that he was not more frightened. It was as if he had been expecting this particular ambush with the troops not firing back, with no one in charge. It was something he had expected to happen for a long time; if anything, his luck had been too good, too many escapes, too many other units ambushed and destroyed and his company barely scratched. It had been as if he were watching the war as a spectator, not as a participant, removed from it with no passion. Indeed his second reaction after the ambush began was a momentary thought whether he should slip over to the other side of the canal and desert. He had watched this entire operation unfold in its singularly stupid way, step by step, stupidity by stupidity. They had walked into a trap set for them, and now they were caught.

He crawled forward toward the center of the column; the further he moved along the more he moved into the range of enemy fire and the more slowly he went. He picked out one machine gun and one BAR and assumed they had supporting lighter weapons as well. He was curious why they had not tripped the ambush with an overwhelming volley of automatic weapons fire and he wondered and worried when the full force of the ambush would begin to show. As he moved forward, he came to the area where the two enemy weapons had converged their fire and leveled his troops. He inched along now, sure that he was going to be hit any minute. He realized now that the tail end of the column had not been badly hit, but what he saw here made him sick, the bodies sprawled out ahead of him. He saw the living pressed into ridiculously thin cover, their faces showing fear and uncertainty, their eyes unwilling to meet his. Just then he heard some fire returned from the front of the column and decided that it was probably the fat American. He passed two enlisted men crouched behind a tree. He yelled out at them to begin firing, and they did not. He yelled again, shouting it as an order, and one answered back, asking where Captain Dang was.

"I am Captain Dang," said Thuong. He took his carbine and fired two shots about a foot above their heads and told them if they did not fire quickly, he would finish the clip on them. To emphasize the point, he fired one more shot into the ground just in front of them. They began to fire, angrily, as if, although they were pointing somewhere else, they were really aiming at him, but gradually picking up the rhythm. He was, he discovered, no longer a spectator, he was engaged; he was making decisions and he wanted to live and to kill.

In front of him was the center of the column where most of the dying had taken place. There was still a soft undercurrent of moans, like background music to the Vietcong weapons and the spasmodic return fire. He saw six young men sprawled out in front, some of them he knew, and some of them he did not. One of them was the soldier he had teased earlier in the day about the medical kit. He knew immediately that if they made it back to My Tho, it would be one of those awful nights when they returned and found that the underground telegraph had sounded and the medical building would be obscured by the great crowd of wives come to be widows, come to wail and claim their dead, and wail even if their men weren't dead. Most of them would be standing there with their children, five and six children perhaps, waiting noisily but patiently outside. They would wait through the night and the next morning they would still be there, outside the battalion commander's office, waiting to have their future explained, what would happen to them, where they should go, how they should live. It was a job which Dang very willingly surrendered to him, and Thuong would explain, interrupting himself for their frequent tears and their breakdowns, that there was no real plan, that they must go home, that there was some money; but if he was to be honest with them, it was sometimes a little late in arriving, knowing that by the time it arrived, it would be so little that it would have all disappeared into debts anyway. The merchants would know which were the wives and the widows and would know just how much credit could be extended. The merchants had been through all this before, and had a good eye for it all.

To the side, as he crawled forward, were three men, still alive, perhaps wounded, but sitting there paralyzed by shock.

"Start firing," he shouted, "start firing now or you'll change places with these others. These were your friends. Don't you care? Don't you care? What are you?"

Ahead of him was the fat American captain kneeling by what must be the young American's body. On his way forward Thuong had been slightly reassured by the sound of firing. The American had at least gotten them to fire a little. But when he saw the Captain, his confidence disappeared. Sweat was pouring down the Captain's face, and his eyes were hard and seemed to be without flex. The Captain's voice was harsh and high, and he was shouting at Thuong.

Thuong let the Captain shout at him for what seemed like several minutes (*the sons of bitches won't fire back; can't you do anything about these sons of bitches; can't you get your damn people to fight; that goddamn Dang has run away, goddamn Army, goddamn country*) before he broke in, trying to calm the man who was after all more or less in charge. He tried to reassure Beaupre about the men and make him forget about Dang.

"I am sorry, Captain," he said, "but I do not think there will be the help for us. I think we are on the own."

The recon patrol came bumbling down the canal path. Ahead there was a small clearing. Out into the clearing they stepped, first one, then two, then finally all eight men. They walked happily across the clearing until they were almost on the other side and about to disappear into the bush again, when the Vietcong, who had been waiting so patiently for the others, finally opened up. The fire was murderous, designed for a much larger party, three machine guns with supplemental BARs, for they had been ready to destroy an entire company and instead they got a squad. Five men were killed instantly, one was wounded, and two were completely stunned, kneeling there, half in the open, not even taking full cover until the Vietcong assault party slipped out of the bushes (this took several minutes because the Vietcong commander at first refused to give the order to clean up the ambush, sensing that it might be a trap and fearing a counter-ambush). Finally he gave the order, and they came out from the canal itself, close enough that if they had missed on their timing, they would have been annihilated themselves. They stripped the dead men, stripped and killed the wounded men, and took the two prisoners with them. They collected the weapons. They were already gossiping with the two prisoners as they left the field. They did not get any automatic weapons.

Along the small canal, Beaupre heard for a brief moment a lull and waver in the Vietcong firing, and then a new outbreak so vicious and violent that he feared that the full waves of the attack were finally about to begin, that it was all over. He saw Thuong quiver; then they both realized that the firing was not there, that it was some distance away on the main canal, and that the recon patrol was being hit. It was very heavy fire, and there did not appear to be any answering fire; then there was a sharp and complete end to it, and they both assumed that all eight men were dead, they *had* to be dead. In that moment Thuong saw Beaupre as more than just a frightened old man in the wrong country and showed him a look of respect. He wanted to say something about the detour, about its giving them a chance, but found he could not.

Suddenly the Lieutenant began to shout something in Vietnamese, angrily, standing up, he was taking risks; Beaupre was sure he would see the man die right in front of him, and for a second thought, *don't stand, you'll pull their fire toward us, toward me*, but the Lieutenant stood, and then moved, shouting angrily at his men, and with a ferocity that Beaupre had never seen from an Arvin officer, steel words coming out of his mouth, like a drill sergeant. They began to fire. A burst came near the Lieutenant, but he only went down momentarily; he was standing again, shaking his fist at two soldiers, screaming. Then as the return fire began to mount, the voice of the Lieutenant began to drop. Goddamn, Beaupre thought, the man is a pistol, we can make it. He was lucky, Beaupre thought, to have a good lieutenant. Three weeks ago Crawford had been with one who had refused to speak English the moment the firing began.

Beaupre went back on the radio, and the CP was friendly and solicitous: "We gonna get something, don't you worry, you stay in there, old buddy, something's gonna be on the way. We just talked to Bien Hoa, and we gonna do it for you, don't you worry."

Beaupre pushed him and was reproved.

"We can't send it any faster than we got it, old buddy. It's all yours, your name on the ticket. Ain't any question of that, it's comin', and now you just stay in there. Get a couple of them for us."

The firing continued around them but the Viets were answering now. The Lieutenant, calmer now, came back and told him that the mortar team had been killed with the first burst.

"Mortars no damn good here, anyway," Beaupre said. He crawled back to the center of death scrounging for weapons, until he found one of the new grenade launchers and decided he wanted it; he hated gimmicks—hated helicopters—but he picked it up and decided it might help. He had trouble at first unwinding it from the limp Asian body. He gathered as many shells as he could for it, picked up another carbine and crawled back to the Lieutenant. He gave the Lieutenant a carbine and a BAR. He asked Thuong to find him one good man. The emphasis was on good. Thuong signaled to a heavyset corporal with a mustache, some kind of tribesman or Cambodian, Beaupre thought. Then Beaupre explained what he wanted: there were two known positions, the machine gun post across the canal and a secondary position somewhere ahead on their side. He wanted the Lieutenant and a few men to keep up a heavy fire until he could work his way back to the head of the column. After that they would keep up the fire and then the Lieutenant would take one or two men, slip further back across the canal, and work the other side: he goddamn well did not want to get caught by another undiscovered position on the far side of the canal.

"The canal," the Lieutenant said, "we will drop some grenades into the canal before we start if it is all right with you. Sometimes they hide in there and we can kill them like the fish."

Beaupre nodded, pleased.

Beaupre took the mustached Viet and began to move slowly, so very slowly, toward the point. He was halfway to the point, a long arduous crawl, around bodies, in blood and slime, when the machine gun opened with a long burst. It sounded so close that Beaupre was sure it was going to hit him, but it missed. It was a few feet behind him, and he turned in time to see it hit the Viet. The man seemed to bounce; he was hit and seemed to stop and hang for a minute, and then he came on. A damn good man, Beaupre thought. They both continued to crawl to the point. Beaupre asked with hand signals if the leg was all right, and the Viet began to laugh. When Beaupre finally reached the point, he realized how exposed he was, and froze again. The smile turned to bewilderment on the face of the Corporal, and it woke Beaupre up. The man was wondering what they were doing there, they were counting on him, and Beaupre remembered again that he was not to freeze, he was to lead. He reached for the grenade launcher.

Thuong turned from Beaupre and began to work his way toward some cover where he could organize his party. On the way he passed Anderson. He crawled a few more yards, and then, turning slowly, and even though he was moving to a less protected spot, moved back toward the dead American. Among the dead, Anderson looked somehow like an adult among children. For a moment Thuong looked at the body and felt no sadness, only justice, let *them* pay too, let theirs die too. Then he caught himself, and was ashamed, and reached over and closed the eyes of the American, and then to his own surprise, started an old Buddhist prayer for the dead; the American, after all, had wanted so badly to be a part of things in this country, he had wanted to share, this was the final sharing. Then he crawled back to a better position and started firing again at the Vietcong.

Beaupre still felt frightened; then the Vietcong

opened with another burst and having survived that, he recovered his nerve again. Below him he heard the firing of the Arvin, steady and surprisingly consistent now. He looked at the grenade launcher and wished now that he had not talked so much against gimmickry, and had shut his mouth and learned to fire the weapon. Raulston had liked it and said it was like a shotgun. He reached down and broke it open like a shotgun. So far so good, he thought. He remembered one thing Raulston had said: don't shoot for them directly, better to shoot in front to get a real effect on the target, and let the scattering take care of itself. He laid eight shells out in front of him, grenades looking like long bullets. He decided that because of the ambush they needed an element of counter-surprise, and he decided to try and make it seem like a semi-automatic weapon. He was sure the VC had never seen one in action. The launchers were new in the country, and he counted on the psychological effect; it was, he was sure now, a small ambush, otherwise they would have been overrun long ago. He was sure they had run into the wings of the main ambush set up to prevent flanking movements. He sighted some trees to the side and in front of the place where he had located the machine gun. He sighted in his own mind the target, so that when he finally aimed, he would be able to fire by instinct and not waste time. He rose with the launcher, fired slightly in front of the target; then, what seemed like clumsy minutes later, his fingers oafish with the tangible effects of his fear, fired again, and hearing the grenades go off, was more confident, firing this time slightly to the right of the pocket.

Behind him now as he fired he heard more noise (were they making more noise, or was he simply hearing it better?) and sensed that the Viets were rallying. He felt some of his fear ebb, and his hands were surer and he pumped two more shells into the pocket. He felt more of his fear ebb and he thanked technology and McNamara.

He knew he had been lucky; the grenades had exploded roughly where he wanted them. He was sure that he had done some damage, but he was just as sure there were some of them still alive, and they could probably still man the weapon. He pumped one more shell in there, in case they were trying to get up. He was sure they had not really come to fight: they had come to ambush, to kill, for a free killing. They were like everyone else, they wanted something for nothing: if there were a new and dangerous weapon used against them they would be very careful. Behind him the Viets were firing now, regularly, almost incautiously. There was no more question of panic.

He heard no more firing from the machine gun position. While he was pumping shells in, it had still been firing, but now it was silent. There was still some firing from the forward position but Beaupre was becoming surer now; he knew the BAR position would hear the silence of the machine gun and he knew it would affect their decisions. He was still not exactly sure where the BAR was. Ahead of him the canal, which was to his left, began to bend to the right. That meant, he thought, that the enemy would not want to be too close to the canal. He did not think they would want the canal as an escape route, it was too easy to dump grenades into the water. They would want to withdraw by land at first, he thought. He and the mustached Viet moved forward, and he began to estimate a place where they might be. About fifty yards ahead was a large clump of bushes. The terrain was too tough, he thought, to ambush the ambushers; perhaps if he had American troops, he might be able to do it, but not with these. He fired a grenade to each side of the clump and listened to the explosions. He thought the second sounded slightly different, more muffled, and then for an instant he thought he heard a muffled human sound, like a man screaming in to himself instead of out to the world. He fired one more to the right of the clump. Then he put down the launcher and picked up a grease gun and a cluster of grenades. He signaled to the mustached Viet and they began to crawl toward the tree clump. The Viet was to the left of him and forward a few yards and Beaupre kept firing to cover them both. It was slow hard work and he was tired now, feeling the tension and the pressure, feeling how incredibly dry he was, dry not like he had been earlier from the heat—he had forgotten about the heat—but dry from fear. He was tired and sick of the whole business. He thought for a moment of standing up and charging the clump. But it would be stupid John Wayne soldiering and he continued to crawl. There was no fire coming from the clump, and when they got within twenty yards, he signaled to the Viet to stop and he lobbed a grenade. He waited, and then because he was an old man and afraid, he lobbed one more. Then he and the Viet slowly rose and walked toward the clump. There they found no men, no weapons, only one tiny patch of blood. Beaupre left the Viet there and walked on a little further; he moved about ten yards ahead and parted some brush and suddenly looked up and saw the enemy, one soldier, wearing black shorts, bare-chested. They looked at each other in total surprise. They were only fifteen yards apart, and in that instant Beaupre saw the carbine at the man's side, saw that his leg was badly wounded, torn up, saw how thin and pitiful and wretched he looked—these are the bastards who do it, he thought, these scrawny goddamn bastards—saw the fear coming on the enemy's face, picked up his weapon and emptied his entire clip into the enemy.

The war was over for the afternoon, he was sure, and he leaned back, exhausted and dry; he found his heart was beating wildly. He positioned the Viet at the clump, went back to the column, and using hand signals, sent three more men up with orders to keep moving in and out of the perimeter. He looked across the canal and waited. Finally he saw the young Vietnamese lieutenant. He shouted for him to work the other side for a few more minutes. The Lieutenant gave him a thumbs-up signal, and Beaupre, surprised at first, grinned and returned it. Go get 'em, buddy, he thought.

He went back on the radio and talked to the CP. The CP was very cheerful and for a moment Beaupre had the feeling that he had telephoned for a disc jockey by mistake. He told them he thought his Victor Charlies were gone for the day. The CP asked how many Victor Charlies he had killed. Saigon, he said, almost apologetically, was anxious to have the results, Beaupre would understand, a bad day and they needed this. Beaupre thought for a minute and said, one and maybe two. The CP asked if he had two or not. Tell them one and maybe two, he said, doggedly, tell them to invent a new category.

"Oh sure," said the CP, "I understand."

The CP told him to wait a minute and then came back happy as ever. They just talked to Bien Hoa, and we got the zoomies back. They're on the way. You want them over there. Bien Hoa's sorry they weren't there earlier, but you can have them just the same.

"No," he said, "but I got a place for them."

"Where?" the CP asked.

He gave the coordinates for the main canal where the recon patrol had bought it.

"You got any observers there?" the CP asked.

"No," he said, "not any more."

"Where you want it?" the CP asked.

"I want it all over the goddamn place. I want it where they were supposed to get us, and I want it north, because they'll probably head north, and you tell the zoomies that if they see anything moving, any mother's sons, white pajamas, black pajamas, no pajamas, to zap their goddamn yellow ass. Anything moves, kill it. I'll take the responsibility."

"Okay," said the CP, "if that's what you want."

"It's what I want," he said.

Behind him the Viets were milling about. Beaupre went back to where Anderson lay, loosened Anderson's canteen and took a long drink from it. He looked through the Lieutenant's papers: he had been twenty-five years old, but had claimed twenty-seven. There was a card showing membership in some West Point group. There was a photo of his young and pretty wife who annoyed Beaupre so much, and a letter which Beaupre looked at, it ended with *love and love, I am feeling so lucky to be married to you even though you're away, I feel the better than the other women even though they have their husbands here.* Beaupre closed it and put the letter in his pocket. He felt embarrassed for having envied Anderson only his decency, his poor decency. He sat down and rested his back against a tree for a minute. Behind him the bark of the tree had been chewed up by machine gun bullets. He looked over and saw the young Vietnamese lieutenant walking toward him. He was walking with a funny expression on his face and then Beaupre recognized it as pain and for the first time Beaupre saw the limp. Thuong came over and sat down next to him, the first time he had ever done that.

"You get hit there?" Beaupre said. "Let's see it."

"No," said Thuong. "I stepped in a punji trap. I was very stupid."

"You'll have to be more careful next time," Beaupre said.

"Yes, next time we must all be more careful," Thuong said.

They sat side by side for several minutes; it was impossible to tell time after a battle, just as it was during a battle, five minutes was five hours, five hours was five days. All time seemed so very long. Finally Thuong, not caring who looked, turned and with great gentleness, started taking off his boot. Beaupre watched, sensing the man's pain. Finally the boot came off. The sole was caked with blood. The foot was absolutely white, a madonna's foot. Beaupre watched him set his teeth and then squeeze the heel.

"We had the good luck," Thuong said to him. "All we hit were the outposts of their ambush."

"Yes," said Beaupre, "the good luck."

He watched Thuong clean the wound and then put the boot back on. Then Thuong went back to the men and started pointing to the dead soldiers. At first there was no response from the living, they did not want to touch the dead. *Do that for them, do that small last thing for them,* Thuong began shouting, and finally the living began collecting the dead. They lined up their dead, and they lined Anderson up too.

Overhead two T-28s flew into view, and began low-flying raids on the main canal; Beaupre could hear the explosions, and he released a purple smoke grenade to mark their own position. They tipped their wings in recognition. Zoomies, Beaupre thought, going back to tell each other what a hell of a war they fought.

By all rights the Viets should have carried Anderson out, but Beaupre, angry with himself, went over and hoisted the body and threw it over his shoulder, smearing his own uniform with the Lieutenant's blood. Thuong continued to shout at the Viets, and one by one they picked up the dead. Then they began to move.

As they moved along, Thuong came over to Beaupre and said the troops were very concerned and worried and they wanted him to talk with the American; they had a question, would there be trucks, or would they have to walk home. They were very concerned.

"We'll ride home," Beaupre said. "Tell them it will all be all right."

On his shoulders the Lieutenant felt heavy and Beaupre lagged behind the others; someone else would have to be the point. Already the Viets were lollygagging again, laughing and talking, even the ones carrying the dead. One more burst of Sergeant Schauss' trusty grenade, he thought, would wipe them all out. He looked at his watch. It was nearly 2 P.M. By three they would link up with the other elements, if they were able to make it, and ride back to My Tho. It was all senseless, he thought. There was no real pursuit, no chase. The VC would reorganize that night and do whatever the hell they wanted. He knew, of course, that by the book some sort of pursuit was mandatory, but he could never get the Viets to pursue now. He could barely get their living and dead asses home; anyway he was tired and glad to be alive, glad that pursuit was hopeless, glad that there was no one there to force him to force the Viets to pursue. They would never find the VCs anyway. He did not want to hunt the VC any more and stay out all night in some tiny village without a mosquito net, being eaten up by the mosquitoes; he wanted to spend the night in the Seminary and sleep between clean sheets, and bitch about the lack of pursuit, and think of the eighteen months he had to go for his twenty.

His war was over for the day and he was glad. It struck him that the Vietnamese lieutenant, Thuong, had been very good, and that he hadn't seen Dang since the ambush. He had finally seen the enemy for the first time; all those months in Vietnam and he had finally seen one. They make a lot of noise for such small people, he thought.

He walked slowly now, a short hulk of a man carrying an immense load, almost more graceful now because of the care he must take as he walked. Big Willian and Anderson in one day, he thought. The VC were getting close. He remembered that he should write to the Lieutenant's wife and visualized the letter, wondering what he could tell her. That her husband had been a good officer, had been desperately in love with her, that he had died during a hot walk in the sun, no not that, he had been killed in a battle, yes, and he wondered where, and thought, Ap Than Thoi, just past Ap Than Thoi, and then he realized it was no good, she knew where Ap Than Thoi was.

Afterword

I WROTE this novel some eighteen years ago. I had been one of the first American reporters to cover the war, arriving in Saigon in the middle of 1962 when there were only 15,000 Americans there. My reporting for the *New York Times* had been well received (except of course by those in high places) and subsequently, after I left in 1964 I wrote a nonfiction book, *The Making of a Quagmire*, about Vietnam.

That was, as they say, a lot of words on Vietnam. But even so there was a part of me which wanted to tell something more, what for lack of a better description, the war felt like on a given day. I wanted to portray the frustrations, and the emptiness of this war. It was after all a smaller and, I think, less tidy war than Americans were accustomed to, and almost nothing that happened in it fit the preconceptions of Westerners. So, starting in 1966 I sat down and wrote *One Very Hot Day*.

It was published in January, 1968 and it received an exceptional early response. The *Saturday Evening Post*, then alive and influential, bought a huge chunk of it. The Literary Guild made it a main selection of the month, a cherished honor. (I remember these details clearly because I was running very short on money at the time and CBS was about to offer me a job as a reporter and the two deals allowed me to remain outside institutional journalism.) *The New York Times Book Review* ran it on page one with a very laudatory review by Wilfrid Sheed, one of our best critics.

It was the most positive send-off one could imagine for a book. Friends who knew the literary market far better than I, assured me that both the book and I were home free. Other reviews were systematically excellent, and even more satisfying, my friends, both military and journalistic who had been in Vietnam, liked the book very much.

Regrettably, however, it never sold very well. Perhaps by then no one wanted to read about Vietnam. Perhaps I, like Lyndon Johnson, had simply been overtaken by events, like the Tet offensive. I have my own suspicion about what happened. I think television's coverage of the war (it was after all, the living-room war in Michael Arlen's phrase) had at least momentarily eclipsed the need for fiction. In World War Two the great war novelists had served a purpose by showing Americans what the young men fighting the war looked like and felt like. Now television, with its startling immediacy was doing that and thereby overnight taking away one of the novelist's traditional functions.

So *One Very Hot Day* passed away. Yet I remain immensely fond of it. A writer's books are I suppose like his children to him; he tries not to play favorites and he loves them all equally. But I retain a secret affection for this book, probably the least known of my works on Vietnam. It still seems to me now, on rereading, what I had wanted it to be when I first wrote it—small and true.

DAVID HALBERSTAM
March, 1984

HEAVY COMBAT

__HOME BEFORE MORNING
by Lynda Van Devanter with   (H30-962, $3.95, U.S.A.)
Christopher Morgan   (H32-153, $4.95, Canada)

This is the story of Lt. Van Devanter, a woman whose courage, stamina, and personal history make this a compelling autobiography. It is also the saga of many others who went to war to aid the wounded and came back wounded—physically and emotionally—themselves. And it is the true story of one person's triumph: her understanding of, and coming to terms with, her destiny.

__CLOSE QUARTERS
by Larry Heinemann   (A31-196, $3.50, U.S.A.)
                                (A31-197, $4.50, Canada)

"This is the way it was . . . the heat, the blood, the terror . . . the taking of pleasure where you could . . . nothing is romanticized, and, finally, nothing is exaggerated . . . which only heightens the horror". —*Chicago Daily News*

__ONE VERY HOT DAY
by David Halberstam   (A32-111, $3.50, U.S.A.)
                                (A32-112, $4.50, Canada)

Within the framework of a single day, this story of a handful of American officer advisors to a Vietnamese infantry company manages to give not only a close-up experience of war but a deeper understanding both of why America was involved and why our mission failed. The time is 1965, before the big build-up of American troops in Vietnam, yet the seed of the future can be found in this book.